# LET THE
# LOVER BE

# LET THE LOVER BE

*by*

## Sheree L. Greer

2014

ISBN 13: 978-1-62639-077-5

This Trade Paperback Original Is Published By
Bold Strokes Books, Inc.
P.O. Box 249
Valley Falls, NY 12185

First Edition: August 2014

---

**Credits**
Editor: Cindy Cresap
Production Design: Susan Ramundo
Cover Design By Sheri (graphicartist2020@hotmail.com)

# Acknowledgments

This novel was a journey in so many ways. Special gratitude to everyone who encouraged, inspired, and cared for me along the way. Thank you Mama, Pops, Tiffany, and Peaches, my award-winning family. Thank you Adella, Amtul, and Don for challenging me to be my best and cheering me on when I didn't think I could make it. Thank you Fiona, Jasmine, and Khaulah for reading my countless drafts, enduring unfounded doubts, and pushing me ever forward to the finish line. I couldn't have done this without any of you. Thank you Iyalorisha Ifatola Adesanya Kerr for helping me light my path. I have so many more people I could name here, people who've nurtured my writing, my heart, and my life, but I'll just say this: may every kindness and gesture of support you grant the world, return to you in abundance! I thank you all. I love you all.

# Dedication

To Jama and Granny: You are not gone.

# CHAPTER ONE

*Friday*

*Stay awake this time. Stay awake this time. Stay awake this time.* Kiana said it to herself like a mantra. Her head swam with snippets of songs, clips of conversation, and a low buzzing noise that was either imagined or real; she didn't know which. Drunk would be an understatement. Kiana had left her friend's party over an hour ago, stumbling to the Blue Line, practically crawling up the stairs to the platform, and finally folding herself into a seat.

The nearly empty train lurched forward. Kiana leaned her head against the window, and though she tried her best to stay awake, she succumbed to a warm, tingling sleep that resulted in her riding the Blue Line "L" Train from the Damen stop to Forest Park and back again. Not exactly back again, but farther back from where she'd even come, no memory of switching to the train on the other side of the tracks. She woke up at O'Hare. Forced to get off the train, she tried to gain her composure before heading back south. She managed to board the train back to the city, chose a seat near the door to stay alert, but dozed off again, drunk and drooling, to Forest Park and back again. The transfers blurred twirls of night air and grimy concrete from one side of the platform to the other, back and forth, to O'Hare as if running line drills.

*Stay awake this time. Stay awake this time. Stay awake this time.* She repeated it. Even saying it aloud. Like Beetlejuice. Three times makes it real. At her third ride to O'Hare, someone caught her arm.

"Are you okay, lady?" the man asked. He wore a gray jumpsuit with his name stitched across his chest. Kiana's blurred vision couldn't make it out, and in her drunkenness, she always called everybody "Buddy," so the kind stranger's name was of no consequence anyway.

"Thanks, buddy," Kiana said, her tongue thick and dry in her mouth. "But I'm good. Just going home." She patted his shoulder. He looked at her skeptically.

Kiana stumbled. The man walked her to a bench. She sat down hard. Her body felt heavy. Like her jeans and coat were lined with that sand they use in ankle weights. She thought about that and wondered if it had a special name.

"It's probably just called sand," she said with a chuckle. She opened her eyes wide, trying to focus, trying to make sense of the bright subway lights and the blurs of blue and yellow and silver that spun around her.

"What did you say?" the man asked, frowning. "Are you sure you're gonna be all right?" He leaned over her.

"I'm good, buddy. I'm good." She waved him off. He walked away, looking over his shoulder at her every now and again as he made his way to the escalator.

When the train boarded to head back to the city, Kiana climbed on, swung her body on the post near the sliding doors, and flung herself into the seat. The car, empty save a petite white woman with a rolling valise twice her size, smelled of burnt cheese. The smell, otherwise putrid and unwelcome on the train car, made Kiana hungry. She looked at her reflection in the dark windows of the train. She ran two hands over her afro, an unruly tangle of coils and kinks jutting up into an inch-thick crown around her head, and stared into her own dark brown eyes.

*Stay awake this time.*

She did.

When the train pulled into the Jackson stop, downtown Chicago, Kiana finally made it off the car and down the stairs, walking in a determined daze through the white-tiled tunnel to the Red Line for her transfer. The musty, dingy halls that lead to the Red Line train held a special kind of quiet. She walked alone, no one singing or clanking cans for change. A couple walking fast and leaning into each other for support, whispered and giggled quietly as they passed her. She made it to the platform just before the doors slid closed. She exhaled loudly then sat in an aisle-facing seat.

A woman with a messy ponytail of tangled fake hair sat across from her, popping her gum and listening to Jodeci on a Discman. "Come and Talk to Me" blared beyond her headphones. Kiana smiled; the woman rolled her eyes. A tall, skinny man in a stretched out Chicago Bulls hoodie pushed through the doors that connected the cars. "Looosies. Loosies. And DVDs,'" he called as he walked up the aisle and through the nearly empty car. A sleeping woman with a cart stuffed with worn Moo & Oink bags sat toward the middle of the car. A woman with two children, both of them wide-awake with runny noses, filled the seats to her left. The woman's head bobbed in exhaustion, her eyes snapping open each time her chin dipped.

Kiana suddenly felt sad. Drunk and sad. She'd been here before. Alone, late at night, on the train, feeling like no one cared about her. Like no one gave a damn. This was the fucked up part about getting loaded. Sure, while drinking and partying, everything is fine. Good times to last you until your last days. That feeling wore off over an hour ago. She had lost the feeling of euphoria somewhere during that last, embarrassing, and ridiculous ride to O'Hare and back.

She closed her eyes. She imagined her friends in bed, the ones she'd just left. They spooned and slept peaceful and warm in the comfort of their North Side flats, all the lights out except for the one over the stainless steel sink of their modern kitchen with marble countertops and breakfast bar. She sighed. She dug in the pocket of her jacket and pulled out her phone. She had a single bar of battery left. She pressed the buttons to get to her recent history. A list of missed calls. None of them from the friends she'd just left. All of them from her sister, Karyn. She'd been calling all day. Kiana called her. She braced herself for her older sister's hard, judgmental voice.

"Kiana?" Karyn asked, her voice hoarse. She cleared her throat. "You know what time it is?"

"No," Kiana said. "What time is it?"

Karyn sighed into the phone. "You're drunk."

"Why you always say that when I call you?"

"I don't know, Kiana," she said. "Why are you always drunk when you call me?"

Kiana shook her head and looked over at the woman with the children, as if she could help her. The train rumbled to a stop at Sox 35th. A man dressed in a faded, stained jogging suit and dress shoes entered the car and sat down. The doors closed and the train pushed on.

"What time is it?" Kiana asked.

"It's after two," Karyn said. She yawned. Kiana didn't know if she was being dramatic or if the yawn was legit. Suspicion and paranoia. Side effects of her lingering drunkenness.

"The Seventy-One still running?" Kiana asked.

"Seriously, Kiana?" Karyn said. "Where are you? Where are you coming from? You on the train?"

Too many questions at once. Kiana was coming down, but she was still drunk. The train stopped. The doors didn't move and there was no overhead announcement. A beep. Another. The train sat unmoving and quiet.

"What?" Kiana said. She shot a confused look to the woman across from her. She nodded to the jam, singing the words under her breath.

"Where are you?" Karyn said, interrupting.

"On the Red Line," Kiana answered. Karyn lit into her. She rambled on about late nights, drinking, transportation, partying on the North Side without a ride home, hanging with white people who don't even really care about you, and drinking too much. Again. It always came back to that.

"What?" Kiana said.

"I said, get off at Sixthy-Ninth and I'll come get you."

Kiana nodded. She closed her eyes.

"Okay?" Karyn said, already shuffling about, getting dressed.

"What?" Kiana said.

"I'll meet you at the stop," Karyn said, ending the call.

Kiana pulled the phone from her ear. She looked at it then slid it back in her pocket. The train began moving again. No announcement, just clicked into gear and continued on. An uneventful stop at 47th, a stop at Garfield that nearly cleared the train, and then 63rd. The woman listening to Jodeci rushed off the train, leaving Kiana all alone. Finally, 69th.

Kiana pushed herself to her feet and made her way off the car and up to the street. She stood at the 71 bus stop. A huddled group of young men in hoodies and oversized jeans stood in the bus shelter passing a single cigarette back and forth. She nodded at them and went to the corner. She looked over at the McDonald's, remembering the smell of burnt cheese on the train. She frowned, but her mouth watered. She stuffed her hands deep in the pockets of her jacket and began walking toward the corner. The restaurant's dark windows didn't register, the muted light of the drive-thru window didn't catch Kiana's eye. She stopped at the corner, the cold wind and blaring streetlights making her eyes water. The glowing arches of the restaurant fought against the shadows of the dim lobby. Kiana couldn't decide if the place was open or closed. She stared at the empty restaurant, licking her lips and trying to remember the last time she had a Big Mac. A car honked short and loud. Kiana jumped and looked over her shoulder.

"Get in the damn car," Karyn said through a crack in the passenger side window.

Kiana stepped toward the rumbling Oldsmobile that nearly ran up on the curb. She leaned over and peered into the passenger window. She cut her eyes. Looking into Karyn's face, she saw herself—the same dark eyes, same pointed chin. She'd come to save herself. A simple smile crept across her lips, a mix of satisfaction and amusement. Karyn honked the horn again, and Kiana jumped.

"Get in the fucking car, Kiana!" Karyn said.

Kiana adjusted her eyes. She recognized Karyn's face, the frown lines around her mouth and deep crinkles at the corner of her eyes. Kiana burst into laughter and looked down at her body as if the absurdity of Karyn coming to rescue her only suddenly became clear. She reached for the door handle and pulled at it. Locked. Her fingers slipped off the handle and she stumbled backward. She laughed and clapped at her thighs.

"How you gonna yell at me to get in and the shit's locked!" She laughed. Holding her stomach and stomping her feet, she looked over at the men in the shelter as if they cared. She reached out for the handle again. Two hollow clicks. Nothing happened. Karyn reached across the passenger seat to flip the lock manually. Kiana, chuckling, finally yanked the door open. She climbed into the car.

"Hey," she said.

Karyn didn't respond. She yanked the gearshift into drive and pulled away from the curb with a screech. She drove in judgmental silence, trying her best to look straight ahead.

Kiana felt Karyn's eyes on her, sidelong glances burning the side of her face and punctuated by irritated sighs. She couldn't face her. Relief and shame wrestled for space in her chest, which burned and bubbled with whiskey and bitters. She gagged and swallowed. Karyn sighed and shook her head. Always the responsible one, the one to take care of things, especially when they were kids, Karyn made Kiana feel safe. But they were adults now. It was time for Kiana to take care of herself. It had been time. Shame took the upper hand.

Drunk and tired, Kiana wiped at the tears burning against her eyelids as Karyn drove down 71st street, the darkened storefronts and vacant lots going by in a blur. Kiana nestled into the passenger seat. The vents blew warm air at Kiana's feet and face. The car smelled of coconut and gasoline. The familiar smell comforted her, and she closed her eyes and nodded out instantly.

❖

Kiana woke up on her couch. She glanced around the small, neat apartment; shadows clung to the small table near the door, the oak shelf filled with books and magazines, and the sagging floor plant. She looked at her sister, who sat crossed in the black leather chair adjacent the couch. She was crossed in every way, crossed as in mad, but also crossed physically, her legs, one bouncing atop the other, and her arms, firm and tight against her small breasts. Kiana had seen the look before, was quite familiar with it, actually.

Without having to guess, Kiana knew she must have been stranded somewhere and needed Karyn to collect her. She closed her eyes to remember, flashes of memory fluttered behind her eyelids: whiskey sloshing and trains clacking, dark tunnels and golden arches. Loosies. Jodeci.

"You're pathetic, you know that, Kiana?" Karyn said. "One of these days, I'm not going to be there to pick you up."

"I'm sorry," Kiana said. She always seemed to be apologizing. She sat up slowly. Her head pounded. She pressed her hands against her temples then smashed her palms into her eyes. Everything was too bright. The lamp next to the chair where Karyn sat, the light coming from the kitchen, the neon green numbers flashing twelve on her stereo. She squinted at Karyn and cleared her throat. "I'm sorry."

Karyn just shook her head. "Whatever." She stood. "This has got to stop," she said.

"I know," Kiana said. She scratched at her scalp through the matted side of her afro. "I said I'm sorry. I just…"

"You just nothing," Karyn said with a shrug. "Look, I saw the invitation."

Kiana winced. She didn't need to look into the other room to see it, the lavender wedding invitation sitting like a strong, elegant tent in the center of her wooden kitchen table. Without seeing it, she could smell it, the vanilla musk whispering from the fold; she could feel it, the heavy cardstock soft against her fingertips as she traced the gold script. She struggled to her feet, the memory of Michelle, of being in love, weighing her down. Though Michelle had been gone just over six months, Kiana ached as if she had just left, as if she just realized that her love was gone for good. "Fuck that invitation," she said, pulling up on her baggy jeans. She walked over to Karyn, who stood in the middle of the spacious living room.

Kiana looked around her apartment, trying desperately not to meet Karyn's eyes. The living room area, exceptionally roomy with the sparse furniture Kiana owned, had often set the stage for private, late night dance parties and indoor picnics for two. Kiana stared at the carpet. Her eyes stopped on the bare space in front of the stereo. A small black cigarette burn marked the carpet. The memory came back instantly, sharp and clear, happening right before her eyes.

Drunk off sambuca and exhausted from dancing nonstop to Gnarls Barkley, Kiana had collapsed on the floor next to Michelle, who lay on her back, smoking a Kool she had bummed from a crinkled, white-haired Jamaican man at the bar an hour before. They had watched the smoke from the cigarette catch the orange glow of the stereo display, curling and twisting, rolling and dancing in the muted light.

"Your energy is astounding," Michelle said, taking a long pull off her cigarette.

"I can't feel my legs," Kiana said. Out of breath and more than a little drunk, she turned on her side. "But I can feel yours," she said, running up Michelle's leg, her fingers sliding up her thighs, finding their way between them.

Michelle turned on her side. With her dancing brown eyes and full lips moist and inviting, her face looked serious, beautiful and serious. She took another drag from her Kool and blew the smoke over Kiana's head. "You can feel a lot more if you want to," she said.

"Oh yeah?" Kiana said. Her hands continued to roam, curving around Michelle's hips and finding her supple ass.

Michelle smiled. "I want you to feel me for real, Key," she said. "The way I feel you." She reached forward, the small piece of cigarette still burning, and placed her hand between Kiana's breasts. "I want you to really, really feel me. Here."

Kiana's heart seemed to pulse against Michelle's hand. She had leaned in, and they kissed. Kiana lost herself in Michelle's lips, like she always did, feeling light-headed, feeling good, so good. The kiss grew, took over them, and in moments, they were both lost. The cigarette forgotten, the glowing butt abandoned in the mix of searching hands, hungry mouths, and aching thighs.

Karen grabbed Kiana's shoulders, shaking her to attention. "Throw it out, Kiana. Don't even think about it." She slid her hands to the sides of Karyn's face. Kiana met Karyn's eyes, and it was like looking into a mirror. She imagined what their mother looked like since Karyn always said they looked like her. Dark brown, doe-like eyes set in a heart-shaped face with full lips and striking cheekbones. Kiana had her father's honey complexion, but any resemblance to the "nameless donor," as Karyn called him, stopped there. Karyn told Kiana that people used to remark how fitting his absence was as it seemed Renee, their young, free-spirited mother, made the girls all by herself.

"Forget about Michelle. Forget about the wedding. Throw the invitation away and focus on you." She looked into Kiana's eyes. She smiled.

Kiana grabbed her wrists and tried to pull her hands down. Karyn resisted.

"I'm serious. Forget about it." Karyn frowned. "You're not as tough as you think you are, you know. I can tell you're hurting."

Kiana tugged at Karyn's wrists. "Don't let this pretty face fool you," she said.

Karyn dropped her hands and crossed her arms.

"I'm as tough as they come," Kiana said. She hardened her jaw against the memory. Michelle had said the same thing before she left, and Kiana had answered the same. Tucking a wavy lock of hair behind her ear, Michelle had looked at Kiana and smiled, whispering in the sweet voice she always used during their pillow talk, "You're not as tough as you think you are." Kiana had smiled through the statement, kissing Michelle rather than challenging what she meant. In retrospect, her leaving the next day had felt like a test. What was supposed to be a summer visit with a group of girlfriends in New Orleans had turned, without warning, into relocation. Michelle hadn't even finished her marketing degree at Roosevelt. Kiana wasn't sure what she was supposed to do, hadn't known what Michelle wanted from her. So as the daily calls turned to weekly check-ins, which gave way to sporadic texts, she tried to steel herself against needing her. She didn't want to seem weak.

Kiana shrugged and adjusted her T-shirt on her shoulders. She spun on her heels, almost losing her balance. "Fuck Michelle."

Karyn shook her head. "Let's get you to bed." She took Kiana's hand and led her to her bedroom.

Kiana undressed, tossing her clothes into an empty laundry basket next to a small pile of sneakers. She slid into her bed. Karyn pulled the comforter over her and up to her chin.

"I'll call you in the morning," Karyn whispered. "I have—" she started then stopped.

"Tell me," Kiana said. She clutched the comforter under her chin. She blinked slowly, the bed spinning beneath her, Karyn's voice soft and soothing.

"I have this place I want us to check out," Karyn said. She sat on the bed. The mattress sagged under her weight. "It's not a rehab, but…"

"But what?" Kiana asked in whisper, her voice and attention fading. Although she didn't feel drunk, the multiple Manhattans she drank earlier that night still lingered just beneath the surface of her subconscious. They danced almost. She felt calm, relaxed. One foot in and one foot out of the moment. She thought of elementary school gym class. Dancing the hokey pokey. She smiled.

"Don't do that," Karyn snapped.

"Don't do what?" Kiana opened her eyes.

"Smile like that. I know what you're thinking. It's not a rehab, I promise. It's just…It's just someone you can talk to. Someone *we* can talk to." Karyn sighed.

Kiana sighed and covered her face with her hands.

"While I was in the kitchen, I saw the wedding invitation, then"—Karyn rubbed Kiana's leg—"I saw all the empty bottles. You should really—"

"Take out my trash more often?" Kiana mumbled.

"No. You should really cut down, and maybe talk to someone. With the way mama—"

"I don't want to talk about that shit now," Kiana said with a groan. She turned on her side to face the single window in her room. The orange glow of the streetlights squeezed through the blinds, stripes of light pressing into the room.

"I know, but we can talk about it together. Say you'll give it a chance. Tomorrow. I'm coming to get you tomorrow. We'll go together."

"Fine," Kiana said.

"Yeah?"

"Yeah." Kiana turned to Karyn and smiled. "Tomorrow. I'll go wherever you want. I'll talk to whoever you want."

Karyn smiled back. She stood then leaned over to kiss her on her forehead. Kiana closed her eyes against the kiss and wouldn't open them again until morning.

# CHAPTER TWO

*Saturday*

Hair of the dog. Kiana chuckled, toasting to the sentiment, alone in her kitchen. She slammed a shot of Maker's Mark and chased it with orange juice. She winced at the bitterness of the juice after the whiskey. She sat at her kitchen table, the just-risen sun blasting through the bay window blinds and her laptop in front of her. A wine-flavored Black and Mild smoked in a makeshift ashtray beside the computer. She picked up the small cigar, rolled the ash against the pickle jar top, then took a long pull. She blew smoke over her shoulder and clicked through her search results. Same day flights to New Orleans. She poured herself another shot of Maker's and sipped it. She took the last swallow from the shot glass and clicked on a flight from O'Hare to New Orleans that left that very afternoon.

She clicked the link for the details of the ticket. She glanced at the invitation. The ticket cost more than she could responsibly afford. She barely made ends meet with her job at New Horizons, a small nonprofit specializing in afterschool programs for kids. She wrote their monthly newsletter and did Web design, or glorified Web updates as she called them, for a few dollars over minimum wage. A few credits short of a bachelor's degree in graphic design from Columbia College, she knew she could do better but always had trouble staying focused, staying committed. Meeting Michelle had changed that, made her look forward to a future that could expunge her past.

"You did all these?" Michelle had asked, looking through her portfolio. "These are amazing! The color, the design." She flipped through the wide pages, logos and websites, mastheads, and billboards full of clean lines, vibrant blocks of color, images that popped off the page.

Kiana had blushed, a response she wasn't used to and rarely succumbed to, and slid the leather portfolio from Michelle's lap. "Thank you," she had said. On her knees in front of Michelle, who sat on the couch, she escaped the moment of embarrassment by doing what she did best. She unbuttoned Michelle's jeans, gripped the sides, and tugged at them.

Michelle had grabbed her wrists, hard. "Seriously, Key, your work is amazing." She searched Kiana's eyes. "You're amazing."

Something about the way Michelle said "amazing" had filled Kiana with a mixture of pride and hope that she hadn't felt in a while. The following week, she set up an advising appointment with her old advisor at Columbia College. She went. She made plans for returning. She got excited by the thought of it all, but when Michelle left, she took all the excitement with her, threw Kiana's hope in her luggage alongside her lace panties and thrift store T-shirts, and never came back.

Kiana reviewed the ticket price and tightened her jaw. *Fuck it.*

She bought the ticket using the emergency credit card she and Karyn shared, the one she promised she wouldn't use without calling Karyn first. Kiana closed the laptop and poured another shot. She situated the Black and Mild in her mouth, clenching it in her teeth and picking up the wedding invitation that sat next to the bottle of whiskey. The invitation was beautiful. Iridescent paper lined with pale pink lace and gold lettering. The playful, sweet scent of vanilla rose from the crease of the invitation and transported Kiana to memories she wished she could forget, moments and experiences she wished she could soak in whiskey and set ablaze, burn into oblivion.

She read the words etched in an elegant font, pressed in gold with delicate strokes and curled ends. "We cordially request your presence for the union of Michelle Denise Matthews and Michael Anthony Freeman…"

*Michelle and Michael. Corny and ridiculous.* Kiana took a shot of whiskey. Her phone rang. Karyn. She pressed ignore and rose from the table. She poured one last shot of whiskey and got busy packing.

Three hours later, her face flushed and body warm and tingling, she jostled along as the Blue Line traveled the all too familiar route to O'Hare. Boarding the plane to New Orleans, she returned Karyn's call. She didn't answer, so Kiana left a message:

"I'm sorry, Karyn. I gotta go though. You know. I mean, it's Michelle. MICHELLE. Michelle, you know. I fuckin'…I fuckin' loved her, you know. I love her. I gotta go, you know. I mean. It's Michelle. Yeah. So, I think…I think we were supposed to do something or talk to somebody. Shit, I don't know. I'm sorry. I'll just…I'll call you when I get back. Oh, I'm going to New Orleans. I have to, you know. So, I'll be there. I'm boarding now. The plane and shit, you know. So, yeah. I'm sorry. She's getting fuckin' married. Tomorrow. Can you believe that shit? Crazy, right? Fuck. Can you go to my place and water my plants? They're gonna need water. I bought this ticket, and I'm not even sure…wait, this lady's asking me for stuff. Wait. Oh no, this is carry-on. Yeah, it fits. Ain't shit hardly in here anyway! Fuck that. Look at that dude's bag. It's bigger than mine. What? Yes. Okay. Thank you. Yeah. What? No. What? Yes. Oh. This is my ticket right here. Ha ha! Yeah. Okay, buddy, whatever. Thank you. Karyn? Sorry. I was…never mind. So, yeah. Water my plants? You always…Oh, shit. Thank you. You know I love you, right? I mean, you…just thank you. Wait. Hold on. Hey, buddy, this is me. 28A. Yeah, over by the window, buddy. Yeah. Karyn. I'm sorry."

## CHAPTER THREE

The elevator door opened directly into the penthouse suite. The scene blew Kiana away. Tall, slender men in white waistcoats and black tuxedo pants walked around with silver trays of colorful, oddly-shaped treats and bubbling glasses of champagne. No one looked in Kiana's direction. The party, in full swing, buzzed with conversation; bursts of laughter rumbled from every corner of the room. The slow whine of a trumpet and hungry grunts of a tuba accented the light, fast-paced groove set by a drummer and pianist in the far corner of the suite. Kiana stood, just outside the elevator doors, which had yet to close behind her.

She searched the small crowds of people, the guests a mixed collection of strangers in fancy strapless gowns and tailored dinner jackets. She took a step forward, and an older white couple, with the most stunning silver hair, looked at her, their sharp blue eyes calculating, evaluating, then dismissing her. Kiana looked down at herself. She adjusted her gray dress shirt on her shoulders. She slid one hand into her black slacks and grabbed a full champagne flute from a tray passing on her right.

Kiana knew Michelle was marrying into money, but she wasn't expecting the embroidered silk sofas and marble statues, the crystal chandeliers, and mahogany bar lined with white leather stools. She remembered a different Michelle, a Michelle who put her last two dollars in the raggedy jukebox at Tom's to play "Stir it Up" five times in a row, a Michelle who, drunk off Malibu and pineapple juice, bought loosie Kools two at a time and always gave one away. Kiana drained the champagne and, before she brought the empty glass from her lips, an attentive server appeared at her side to offer her another. She replaced her empty glass with a new one, nodding her thank you. She sipped this one, letting the tart bubbles dance on her tongue. She wandered through the grand space, looking around, smiling a tiny smile at the few people who looked at her for more than a second.

Kiana circled the entire party and found her way back to the bar. She placed her empty champagne glass on the shiny mahogany surface. The bartender, a redheaded man with a ruddy face and aquamarine eyes, wiped the inside of a glass and winked at her. She leaned forward to order a drink when she heard it:

Michelle's laugh.

Michelle's laugh, energetic and bright, exploded in the air, and floated down like confetti. Kiana turned. Michelle stood a short distance away, ten feet at the most, one hand on her hip and the other resting on the shoulder of a short, balding white man with a bushy moustache, who obviously said something absolutely hilarious. He gestured with his hands and Michelle laughed again, just as loud and carefree and beautiful as before. Kiana's mouth went dry. Michelle was stunning.

An emerald green dress caressed every slope and curve of her body. The bodice, corset-like and fashioned with black lace, held her cinnamon brown breasts up and out. Her hair, which she used to wear wild and curly, was straightened and swept up into an elegant bun, from her neck to her shoulders, every line of her body a graceful and intentional invitation to admire God's most beautiful creation. Michelle laughed again. Quieter this time, but no less intoxicating. The bartender cleared his throat, and Kiana turned to him, panicked. Suddenly terrified and anxious, she took a deep breath and licked her lips.

"Can I get you something?" he asked, smiling.

Kiana couldn't find her voice, but she heard Michelle's. She glanced over her shoulder as Michelle, her voice clear and bright as ever, introduced herself to the couple with the silver hair. The woman asked to see the ring. Michelle held out her hand. The woman took her hand and nudged her husband, who shielded his eyes with his hands, exaggerating only slightly. Even from where Kiana stood, the shine of the large diamond was impressive. The three of them continued to chat about the wedding plans for the week.

"The week?" Kiana whispered to herself.

"What's that, lovey?" the bartender said.

"I thought the wedding was tomorrow," she said.

"No, ma'am. A week from today," he said. "I'm working the reception," he added with a proud smile.

Kiana sighed and shook her head. Her mind reached back to the invitation, trying to remember the dates. All she could recall was Michelle and Michael. Union. Sunday. She frowned and continued watching Michelle entertain the distinguished looking couple. When the man inquired about the whereabouts of her fiancé, Michelle smiled graciously and said, "Oh, my Michael will be here soon. He had an unexpected business call."

*My Michael.* Kiana swallowed hard, her heart pounding in her ears.

"Miss? Can I get you something? It's an open bar. Name your poison," the bartender said behind her.

Kiana needed a drink, but she couldn't take her eyes of Michelle. It was good to see her, and she hated every second of it. As much as she wanted to go over to her, shove the silver-haired couple out of the way, and stand directly in front of her, to ask her questions and demand answers, Kiana also wanted to disappear. In direct contrast to Michelle's firework laughter that exploded overhead in bright, vibrant light, she wanted to implode into darkness, into nothing.

The couple brought Michelle into a hug, and when she turned her head to offer her cheek to the silver-haired gentleman, she saw her. She finally saw her. Michelle met Kiana's eyes, and Kiana, as if suddenly aware that flying down to New Orleans to confront her ex-lover meant actually confronting her ex-lover, turned around in a panic, trying to steady herself. Deep breathing didn't work. She squeezed her fists at her side.

"What will it be?" the bartender asked again, forcing a smile through his obvious irritation.

"Maker's. Neat," Michelle said over Kiana's shoulder. She slid next to her, smiling.

"You remember," Kiana said, nearly choking on her breath and startled at how quickly Michelle had made her way over to the bar. "You actually remember," she said again. She steeled her lips before a smile could form. She didn't want to smile at her, for her. She was sure Michelle could remember lots of things about her, but what did it matter if she could walk away and so easily?

"How could I forget?" She smiled, her shapely lips framing even white teeth, eyes brown and playful.

Kiana wanted to say something, wanted to let Michelle know how the sting of her leaving and the ache of six months without her returned anew each day. She began to speak then stopped.

The bartender slid the drink to her and nodded toward Michelle. "And you?" he asked.

"Nothing for me." She waved her hand to decline. "I've had too much champagne already," she whispered to Kiana.

Kiana rolled her eyes. "You always were a lightweight." She took the drink the bartender poured, raised it in salute, and knocked it back, almost draining it. She stared down at the sip of brown liquid left in the glass, instantly wanting a refill. She licked her lips and took a deep breath.

"Rather that than a lush," Michelle said. They stared at each other. The bartender noticed the tension and backed away slowly, turning his attention to a woman sipping from a nearly empty wine glass.

"A lush?" Kiana nodded. "You know—"

"I didn't think you would come," Michelle interrupted. "Actually, I was pretty sure you wouldn't."

"Is that why you invited me? Because you thought I wouldn't come?" Kiana twirled her glass slowly. It seemed just the nonsensical type of thing Michelle would do, compiling her list of wedding guests, thinking of Kiana then jotting her name down with a shrug. That's the way she had been with their relationship, doing things, saying things just because, an attitude of carelessness and daring with no thought of the consequences. In the beginning, it was attractive, exciting even, but it quickly incensed Kiana as she pressed Michelle to make decisions about their relationship, about their future.

"No." Michelle shifted. "I invited you because…because I miss you. I miss our friendship."

"Friendship?" Kiana lifted her glass and drank the last of the whiskey. "You've got to be fucking kidding me."

"Really. I thought that inviting you would be like, I don't know, burying the hatchet. Starting over. We didn't end things on the best of terms." Michelle put her hand on Kiana's thigh. She looked at her and smiled. "We should…"

"We should what?" Kiana said. She glanced down at Michelle's hand in disgust, the shining engagement ring screaming up at her. Michelle moved her hand. Kiana looked over her shoulder at the party, reminded of the occasion by the blaring ring and smiling guests.

"I didn't end things at all," she said. "So there's no 'we,' Michelle. There's only you. Only what YOU did," Kiana said raising her voice.

"Let's not place blame," Michelle said in a hushed voice meant to calm Kiana down. "You came, right? That means something."

The conversation wasn't going the way Kiana had planned. Then again, she hadn't had a plan. Only an impulse, a need to quell the pain, the ache. An ache that not only didn't go away when Michelle never returned to Chicago, but worsened, from dull aching to relentless throbbing the second she received the lavender envelope with her name scrawled in elegant script. She hated the way she felt. She hated Michelle. And she loved her.

"Fuck you, Michelle," she said.

"Come on, Kiana. Don't be like this. It's obvious you've been drinking and—"

"And what? What the fuck does that have to do with anything?"

"You know how you get when—"

"No. I don't know how I get. Tell me how I get." Kiana slammed her empty glass on the bar. "I want to know. How the fuck do I get?"

The bartender made a move toward them. Michelle lifted her hand to wave him off and smiled at him. She looked around at the party then cut her eyes at Kiana. "You're making a scene."

"A scene? Fuck—"

"There you are!" a man called out. He walked over to Michelle and Kiana with a grin. Tall and thin, he moved gracefully toward them. His eyes, warm and sweet as brownies, flashed at Kiana then settled on Michelle. He grabbed her up in a one-armed hug about the waist, pulling her protectively into his lean, athletic body. He held Michelle with confidence, and his complexion, the dark, commanding brown of Colombian Roast, made his bright, wide smile all the more disarming.

Kiana bit at the inside of her jaw. The man, who Kiana assumed had to be the fiancé, kissed Michelle's forehead. Michelle smiled up at him.

"The second I walked in," he said, "I was instantly bombarded with all sorts of questions and congratulations. It was insane! All I wanted when I got off that call was to see your face. Turns out, you ditched all the schmoozing for the bar. Who's your friend?" He nudged his chin toward Kiana.

"Michael, this is—" Michelle began.

"Nobody," Kiana said. She quickly dug into the pocket of her slacks and took out a small billfold. She thought, in a split second, how nice it would be to punch them both in the face. "I'm nobody," she said before Michelle could speak. She couldn't bear to hear her voice any longer. She peeled a five-dollar bill from her fold of cash and laid it on the bar. She tapped it, shook her head at the couple, and turned away to leave.

"It's an open bar, you know," Michael said.

Kiana stopped and looked over her shoulder. Michael smiled, his arm wrapped around Michelle's waist, the gesture casual but complete in its ownership and propriety. Michelle leaned into her man, her eyes betraying nothing, her face stoic. Kiana bit at the inside of her cheek and shook her head, a helpless gesture that seemed the only fitting response, and made her way to the elevator.

She pressed the button and the doors slid open instantly. She stepped inside and slumped against the back of the wall of the elevator. Michelle and Michael had already left the bar and disappeared into the congratulatory smiles and open arms of their guests.

Another drink. Kiana needed another drink. Many more drinks, actually. She thought briefly of the open bar she'd left, and the ease and immediacy with which the bartender supplied her with whiskey. A quick pour. No other expectations and no judgment. She shouldn't have left, but she had no idea what to say to Michelle and most certainly didn't know how to face "her Michael." The sight of them together made her sick. Her face burned, and her stomach tightened into a hard ball of muscle. It hurt.

She unbuttoned the third button of her dress shirt, suddenly flushed and tingling with frustration. She spotted a puddle in the corner of the elevator. Kiana hoped it was water and not piss. It was clear, and it didn't smell. Definitely, probably water. Or a cocktail. A spilled vodka tonic or vodka press. The inside of Kiana's jaws moistened. The elevator door opened on the fourth floor, and an old white man in an expensive suit entered, his cheeks flushed red with intoxication and his hands clutching a Collins glass of amber liquid. Kiana cut her eyes at him for no other reason than he had a drink and seemed happy, a simple smile on his face as he glanced over at her. He stepped to the corner of the elevator and stood in the vodka-tonic-maybe-water-possibly-piss. Kiana grinned.

When the elevator dinged and the doors opened, the cool air of the lobby filled the small space instantly. The white man held his hand out for Kiana to exit. She returned the gesture; the white man chuckled and stumbled out. Kiana followed.

The lobby was bright and bustling with late night activity. Drunken cliques of blond white girls walked across the lobby bumping each other's shoulders, laughing and yanking down on their too tight, too short spandex dresses. A few of them carried their strappy stilettos, the sling-backs hanging from the hooks of their index fingers, others braved the walk across the carpeted floor on trembling legs. There were groups of men, ties loosened and suit coats askew, polo shirts damp with sweat and plastic drink cups in their hands. Everyone drunk. Kiana looked at her watch. It wasn't even ten p.m. Kiana stopped staring and joined in the fray.

She made her way out into the street and a few doors down to another hotel with a lobby just as busy. She walked over to the bar and ordered a Maker's neat. She drank it quickly, the burn just what she needed to right herself. She ordered another. Looking around as she sipped the second drink, she tried to get a handle on the night. What she was even doing there. What she was going to do next. She motioned for the bartender.

"You ready for another one already?" he asked. "You better pace yourself, baby. The night is young and full of life. You are young and full of life. Too many, too fast will mess with both of dem, yes?" His accent was Bayou thick.

"I have a question," Kiana said, drinking her whiskey down. "I'm not from here."

"I figured that," he said. He flashed a toothy grin and leaned on the bar.

"Well, I'm looking to have a good time," she said. She tapped her empty glass. "One more while we talk."

The bartender shook his head and spun around to grab the Maker's. He poured Kiana another drink.

"A good time?" the bartender said, sliding the half-filled glass toward Kiana. "You're in N'Awlin's, and good times is our specialty. Big Easy as they say!" He winked. "Now, a smooth character like yourself," he began, considering her with a sidelong glance, "should be out among the beautiful people."

Kiana smirked and adjusted the collar of her shirt. "Oh, you think so?" she said. She rolled up her sleeves. She felt comfortable in a way she wasn't used to when in a new city. She looked around. The collection of people, elegant and plain, men and women, straight and gay, struck her for the first time. Two women in evening gowns and tuxedo jackets walked gracefully to the elevator. A small group of men, outfitted in stylish suits and fedoras cackled and slapped at each other's arms in laughter. A young couple in matching khaki shorts, polo shirts, and name tags sat at the bar whispering and giggling in a dark corner. A tall man with a feather headdress and sequined halter top leaned against the bar and fished through his pocketbook, finally pulling out a half-smoked cigar and Zippo lighter. The Big Easy indeed. Everyone seemed so at ease in their skin, so contented in their identities that Kiana wanted to buy the lot of them a round of drinks.

"Who you here with?" the bartender asked.

Kiana took a slow swallow of her whiskey. She pressed her lips against teeth. "Just me, myself, and I, buddy."

"No," the bartender said with exaggerated shock. "That ain't right!"

"Whether it's right or not, it's the truth." Kiana shrugged and sipped her drink. "I'm all I got, buddy. I'm all I got."

The next few drinks went by in a flash, and when Kiana hit the street, the Maker's she slammed at the bar came down upon her, heavy and soft as a velvet curtain.

The Quarter was a blur of bodies and sounds. She couldn't make out faces, but she could see the music. Waves of magenta flowing from unseen trumpets, goldenrod bursting from invisible saxophones, and cerulean blue overflowing from phantom pianos. The music glowed in the darkness of the night. She walked in what she hoped was the general direction of her hotel. She bumped her way through small groups of people, partiers headed to the next bar, lovers headed to their rooms. She pushed her way to a corner and stood. Just stood. Staring. The streets were alive with eyes and teeth, music lighting the way. Lost and woozy, she took a step off the curb. A hand caught her about the elbow.

"Watch yourself," a woman's voice said.

Kiana yanked her arm from the woman's grip. "I've got it!" she said over her shoulder. She stumbled, swaying on her feet. A sheet in the wind.

The woman frowned and took Kiana gently about the shoulders. "Are you all right?"

"Yeah," Kiana said. "I'm fine, buddy." She slumped in the woman's arms.

# Chapter Four

*Sunday*

Kiana woke up cold. She held herself and shivered awake. She opened one eye and looked around the small, sparsely decorated room. A tall, mahogany bureau stood against the wall, and small tables, both covered with a red cloth etched with gold eddies, flanked the bed. She squinted toward the single window, sunlight muted against the sheer, off-white curtains. She sat up, holding the side of her head. A dull ache pounded against her right temple. Still intoxicated, she licked her lips and then her teeth, where a bitter film met her tongue. She grimaced and forced herself to swallow. She looked down at herself.

Kiana still wore her clothes from the night before, pants and tank top intact, her button-up shirt lay at the foot of the bed. Good. She looked around the room. She had no idea where she was. Bad. She cleared her throat and swung her legs over the side of the bed. Her bare feet against the cool hardwood sent a quick chill through her bones, yet the solid cold of the floor stabilized her. Made her feel alert. A bucket sat next to the bed. Empty, but ready. Kiana chuckled. She hadn't thrown up from drinking in ages. She licked her teeth and smacked her lips.

Stale whiskey. She closed her eyes and tried to remember the night before. The door opened behind her, and she turned.

"You're awake," a woman's voice rang out from the doorway. The woman, about Kiana's height but thinner and more toned, leaned against the doorjamb. She wore fitted jeans and a white v-neck T-shirt that hugged her small, braless breasts. She held a glass of orange juice in one hand and ran the other through her short, curly black hair. She smiled. Her skin was pale as uncooked plantain and her eyes were too light to be called brown, but too dark to be considered hazel. "I'm Genevieve. But most people call me V." She sipped her juice.

"Good morning, Genevieve. I'm Kiana." She smiled back.

Genevieve raised an eyebrow.

"I'm not most people," Kiana said. She pushed herself up from the bed with a slight grunt, her body aching with hangover dehydration. She turned to completely face her Good Samaritan, who smiled at her with the most genuine gesture Kiana had witnessed in a long while. Genevieve was gorgeous but seemed unaware of it. As if her face was just her face, not stunning or remarkable, just an arrangement of eyes, nose, and mouth.

"Obviously," Genevieve said.

"How so?"

Genevieve drank from her juice then licked her lips. "You're calm and at ease. Not panicked. You used to waking up in strange places?"

Kiana narrowed her eyes and pursed her lips. "Shit happens." She shrugged and pushed her hand through the thick, matted coils of her afro. "Besides, I've got a guardian angel." She smiled and smoothed her pants and grabbed her shirt from the foot of the bed. She put it on and started buttoning it up. "I do thank you though. I'll be out of your way in a second." When she finished adjusting her shirt, she patted her pockets for her phone.

"It's in the front room," Genevieve said. She spun off the doorjamb and walked down the short hall. Kiana followed, using her fingers to pick out her hair at the back and the sides. The front room, warm and bright with sunlight, was neat, but a bit cluttered with paintings on every wall, huge clay pots and figures lining walls and squatting in corners, and varieties of house plants. Kiana squinted against the sunlight, a dull ache spreading across her forehead.

Genevieve nodded toward the cocktail table, a wooden table covered with the same red cloth from the bedroom tables. Atop the table sat Kiana's cell phone, a small fold of twenties, and her room key. She walked over to the table and swiped up her belongings. She looked at Genevieve, who stood in the kitchen, a small area separated from the rest of the living space by nothing but a small breakfast bar with two stools.

"By the door," Genevieve said. She gestured past Kiana.

Kiana turned. Her black leather loafers, neatly situated side-by-side, sat next to a clay umbrella holder shaped like a woman's torso. Two umbrellas, one purple and one black, and a crooked walking stick jutted out from the slopes of the woman's shoulders and chest where her head should have been. She looked at the shoes then back over her shoulder at Genevieve. She raised her eyebrow. It was as if Genevieve were reading her mind, anticipating her questions. Her head still swam a bit, and Genevieve's calming sense of control made her uncomfortable.

"Thank you," Kiana said. Her voice cracked, her throat sore and dry from too many shots. She walked over to her shoes, slipped her feet into them, and turned to face Genevieve. She coughed into her hand and cleared her throat. Her stomach churned and her head throbbed.

"Want some juice?" Genevieve asked. She didn't wait for an answer. She went into the refrigerator and took out a clear pitcher a quarter full of orange juice. "I squeezed it myself."

Kiana walked across the living room and stood between the two stools. "Thank you," she said. She took the glass of juice Genevieve slid toward her. She sipped it slowly. Cold, sweet, and thick, the juice coated her throat, soothing it where the whiskey had burned it raw.

"It's good." Kiana drank more. "Wouldn't happen to have any vodka, would you? Hair of the dog?" She sipped and raised her eyebrows, smiling.

Genevieve shook her head. "Sorry. Can't help you." She poured herself more juice.

Kiana sighed. She looked around the kitchen. Her eyes caught a chain of wishbones and dried chili peppers hanging beside the small window over the sink. "You're one to talk, you know," she said.

"What?" Genevieve paused, her glass of juice hovering at her full lips.

"You're calm. At ease." She tilted her head and cocked an eyebrow. "You used to bringing strange women home?"

Genevieve laughed. She placed her glass on the breakfast bar without taking a sip. "Shit happens," she said, leaning on the counter. "And," she continued with a smile, "I got a guardian angel, too." She chuckled softly.

Kiana drank the last of her juice. Under different circumstances, she might have liked Genevieve. She smiled at her. "Yeah, I bet." She adjusted her shirt, started to tuck it in, then stopped with a shrug. Fidgety and suddenly irritated, she clenched her fists at her side and took a deep breath. "I'm gonna go. You've been very nice, and I appreciate you taking me in last night. I'm sure I was a mess. I'm sorry if I did anything or said anything…" She paused, giving Genevieve a chance to tell her a little about the night.

"Blackouts," Genevieve said, not taking the bait. She whistled and shook her head. She looked up at Kiana then sipped her juice.

Kiana sighed and turned away from Genevieve. She walked toward the door, pulling her phone out of her pants pocket. She stopped.

"You can use mine," Genevieve said. She joined Kiana in the front room, walked over to the old desk in the corner of the room, and unplugged her phone from the charger. She handed it to Kiana. "I was wondering if you had someone to call."

Kiana stared down at the phone. She started to dial then stopped. "You know the number for a cab?"

"A cab?"

"Yes. A cab? A taxi? Taxicab? Whatever you call it down here." She held the phone back out to Genevieve expectantly.

"So you really are here all alone?"

"Yes," Kiana said. "So what? Women can't travel alone? What year is it?"

Genevieve held her hands up defensively and took the phone. "I just…it's just strange that you're down here by yourself. Most people come down with friends, with lovers." She shrugged. "Being here alone, I would think you'd be more careful. When I found you, you were tore down."

"You didn't 'find' me," Kiana said. "You bumped into me. I would've made it to my hotel. It wasn't far from where I was."

"How would you know?"

"Look, can you just call me a cab so I can get out of here?" Kiana crossed her arms and tapped her foot. She didn't appreciate Genevieve's attitude. Being beautiful didn't give her the right to be an asshole; plus, she could have really used a drink. Something to take the edge off. Her head still throbbed, though less intensely.

"Where you staying? I asked you last night and tried to tell from your room key, but…"

"At the Holiday Inn."

"On Royal?"

Kiana scrunched her face. "Yeah, I guess. Near the Quarter."

Genevieve chuckled. "That's not far from here," she said. "I can give you a ride." She slid her phone into the pocket of her jeans and walked back over to the desk. She grabbed a small leather messenger bag and slid her feet into the canvas sneakers next to the desk chair.

"You've done enough," Kiana said. "Really."

"It's nothing," Genevieve said. She opened the door and held it open for Kiana to walk through.

Kiana squinted against the sunlight, the brightness of the day irritating her just as much as Genevieve's attitude and mind reading. The irritation didn't hold as she followed behind Genevieve through a small garden with a babbling fountain. The beauty of the flowers and foliage dulled the sharpness of her attitude. She slowed her steps and looked around.

"It's pretty out here," she said quietly, more to herself than anything else. The garden burst with color, wide bushes with red blossoms, tall plants with yellow flowers, and moss hanging from dipping tree branches.

"Thank you," Genevieve said. "I do some of the gardening." She stopped and surveyed the greenery before walking up a narrow cement path past the main house and onto the sidewalk and one-way street. "My landlord does most of it though. When she's here." She shrugged and walked up to a bike chained to a large tree. She stopped.

Kiana looked around, waiting. A few cars and scooters lined the street. Kiana surveyed the vehicles, trying to guess which one belonged to Genevieve. When Genevieve stepped closer to the locked bicycle, reaching out to yank the chain away from the tree, Kiana shook her head.

"You're out your fucking mind," Kiana said. She pointed at Genevieve's bike. "You expect me to get on there?"

"Yes," Genevieve answered. She looked at Kiana without blinking. "What's the matter?"

"You don't offer people a ride when all you got is a bike. You're insane."

"It's transportation," Genevieve said.

"Yeah, but it's a bike." Kiana scrunched her face then looked Genevieve up and down. "What I look like letting you pump me on your bike? I'm a grown woman. And you...you're so..."

"Baby, I'm as tough as they come," Genevieve said. She put her hands on her narrow hips.

Kiana's throat clutched. She swallowed hard, her mind seeing Michelle's face and remembering the last night they shared in Chicago. She hadn't thought of her all morning.

"Sure you are," she said, finding her voice and shaking off the memory. "Me, too. Which is why I am not getting on that bike with you."

"Oh," Genevieve said. She looked Kiana up and down then nodded. "I should have figured you were one of those."

"One of those?" Kiana held her arms out and looked down at her wrinkled dress shirt and slacks. "One of what?"

Genevieve smirked. She poked out her chest and snarled. "One of those big bad studs who ain't gon' ride on a bike like a punk," she said, lowering her voice and squaring her shoulders. She exhaled and smiled.

Kiana laughed despite herself. The "stud" reference surprised her. She'd been called a stud before, but never resigned herself to the label. She was more surprised that Genevieve had used the term at all, the ease of reference told Kiana what she hadn't thought to ask. She smiled, feeling a quick sense of welcome and belonging.

Kiana cleared her throat. "That impression or whatever that was supposed to be was terrible. Look, I just don't think…" She gripped the handlebars of the bicycle. Sunlight glinted on the bell of the horn attached near the left handle. Vintage and well-maintained, the bike's frame, the striking, bright green of radioactive peas, revealed neither rust nor scratches. The bike was loved and it showed. "It's just not what I expected, and I'm sure you're very strong, but…" She frowned.

"It'll be easy. I guarantee." Genevieve unlocked the bike and quickly wound the chain around the base of the seat.

Kiana looked around the empty, quiet street. Genevieve had called her out, and she had never been one to back down from a challenge. She took a deep breath. "All right. Tell me what to do," she said.

Genevieve clapped her hands and got on the bike. She steadied it between her legs. She directed Kiana with her hands, moving her toward the front tire and telling her to straddle it. The large, rectangular reflector nudged her ass. Genevieve grabbed Kiana's waist. Kiana stiffened.

"Relax," Genevieve said.

"I'm trying to," Kiana said. She leaned back, gripping the handlebars with trembling hands.

"On three, hop up on the handlebars," Genevieve said.

"I don't know about this," Kiana said.

"One, two, three!" Genevieve lifted as Kiana hopped back onto the handlebars with an awkward squeal. Before Kiana's butt settled, Genevieve expertly shifted her hands to the rubber handlebar grips to steady the bike.

Kiana's chest heaved and she laughed, feeling silly. She looked over her shoulder. The bike wobbled as Genevieve walked it forward a few steps, getting used to Kiana's weight on the front of the bike. Kiana snapped her head forward, letting out another little scream. She readjusted her grip on the warm metallic handlebars of the classic Schwinn.

"Just sit still," Genevieve said. "Don't lean back or to the side. Just sit and let me and the bike guide the way." She pushed the bike forward with her legs. "And most importantly, relax. We'll stay on the banquette for a little bit then go into the street real easy." She grunted softly and pressed the bike forward. Kiana instantly felt unsafe, insecure, teetering on disaster. Genevieve pedaled the bike up the sidewalk a ways and finally into the street. The bike moved smoothly, Genevieve keeping perfect control and balance as her legs found a rhythm.

"You okay?" Genevieve asked, leaning forward slightly to talk over the wind and look around Kiana's body and up the street.

"Yes," Kiana lied, her voice shaky. She gripped the handlebars beneath her buttocks and tried her best to relax like Genevieve said.

It wasn't working. If she were drunk, she wouldn't be worried; she'd be smiling, laughing even, might have even raised her hands over her head and yelled "Wooooohoooo!" But she was sober, the last shadows of whiskey having been chased away by the late morning sun.

Genevieve noticed the uneasiness in Kiana's voice and moved the bike opposite the parked cars that lined the tight, one-way street. She picked up a little speed, the faster the bike moved, the smoother the ride, the more balanced the bike. She leaned ever so slightly, looking around Kiana's body to turn and steer up a side street.

They passed a bustling café, the large windows offering a peek at the customers inside sipping hot drinks and eating pastries, laptops and newspapers set before them. There were boarded up storefronts, the wooden slats a patchwork of peeling stickers and colorful flyers. A man chaining his bike to a pole outside a corner bookstore waved at the two of them before standing and turning his attention to the tables of books and records spilling from the store's open door to the street.

The air smelled sweet; the aroma of fresh baked bread hit Kiana full on as the bike came up on a bakery. A man pushed a metal cart of covered bread toward a small white delivery truck. He nodded at Kiana and Genevieve as they passed. Kiana smiled; her body loosened. The delicious breeze, the smiling, welcoming faces, and Genevieve's smooth, rhythmic pumping, the bike gliding, it all filled her. She relaxed, her hands tight on the handlebars but no longer aching in their effort. She smiled and closed her eyes. She wobbled through memory, searching for balance, something solid and good to match the moment. She tried to remember the last time she'd been on a bike.

"Go faster," Kiana whispered. The wind swallowed her voice. "Go faster," she repeated.

"What?" Genevieve said, hunching forward as she looked around Kiana's arm.

Kiana opened her eyes and carefully yelled over her shoulder, "GO FASTER!"

Genevieve pedaled harder. "Here we go!"

Kiana laughed, smiling and closing her eyes against the blur of street. Memory seized every part of her. Her heartbeat, her breath, her gripping fingers, every part of her became pulses of memory. No clarity or continuity, her memory existed in flashes, fragments of history: Her mother. The nape of her neck and the round of her shoulders. The curve of her back. The light catching her gold hoops and the copper coils of hair sneaking out from the scarf tied around her head. Kiana watched the slight movements of her shoulders, the watchful head turns as she rode them through the neighborhood. Kiana clapped her little four-year-old hands, still sticky from the Popsicle she'd slurped early into the ride. She smiled. She opened her eyes, the bike slowed to a stop.

"Should probably get off and walk the rest of the way," Genevieve said, slightly out of breath. She held the bike steady. Kiana slid off the handlebars slowly, wiping her eyes.

"The wind," she said. "Could have used goggles or something."

"Yeah, you right," Genevieve said. "That wasn't too bad though was it?" She nudged her chin up the street to signal the direction they needed to start walking. They were about two blocks from Kiana's hotel. People walked the streets carrying shopping bags and stopping at windows and vendors that lined the street. Cars blaring music zoomed through yellow lights; a streetcar rambled to a stop.

"Not at all," Kiana said. She took a deep breath and shook herself from the memory of good times, forcing them deep inside lest they conjure up darker memories. "It wasn't bad at all."

"Don't worry," Genevieve said. "I won't tell anyone. Would hate for your stud card to be revoked." She laughed and bumped Kiana's shoulder.

"Whatever," Kiana said. "I'm not into all that. I'm just me."

Genevieve rolled her eyes. "Baby, you won't survive down here with that 'I'm just me' talk." She laughed.

"Luckily, I don't need to survive down here," Kiana said. "I'll be heading back to Chicago soon."

"Yeah, you right," Genevieve said. She dropped her head then shrugged. "I suppose it don't matter then."

"You can still keep that bike thing between you and me though."

Kiana and Genevieve looked at each and shared a laugh. They made their way to the hotel, Genevieve walking the bike between them. Kiana told Genevieve why she was in New Orleans. She didn't mention her history with Michelle, saying only that she was in town for a wedding.

"Oh," Genevieve nodded. "How long are you here for? When's the wedding?"

"What's today?" Kiana said, half-serious.

"Sunday."

"The wedding is in exactly one week," Kiana answered with a sigh. She shook her head, recalling the conversation she'd overheard at the cocktail party, Michelle gushing about the week's activities leading up to the wedding: brunches and rehearsal dinners, spa days and bachelorette parties. She couldn't afford to stay, but she couldn't leave without talking to Michelle. Her mission came rushing at her, a wave of emotion that would knock her over where she stood if she wasn't careful. She squared her jaw and made a quick decision to stay, credit card and savings be damned. She knew Karyn would call, worried and furious, but she hoped Karyn would understand. She bit her lip and looked at Genevieve.

"There's a bunch of planned activities and what not. It's a big deal," she said.

"A week," Genevieve said. They reached the hotel. "So I have you for a few days then?"

"Excuse me?"

"So you have a few days then?"

"That's not what you said," Kiana said. She fought a smile.

Genevieve fingered the curve of her bike's handlebars. She looked down at the bike then up to meet Kiana's eyes. "I'd like to see you again," she said.

"You don't even know me," Kiana said. "You might not like me much once you do." She shifted, staring at her feet. She looked up the street and noticed a liquor store a few shops from the corner.

"Let me be the judge of that." Genevieve smiled. "Baby, I don't believe in accidents or coincidences. I found you for a reason."

"You didn't find me."

"Right." Genevieve laughed. "I bumped into you for a reason."

"Fine," Kiana said. She watched a man dip into the liquor store.

"Tomorrow. I'll meet you here. Noon."

Kiana smirked. "You're different."

"Why you say that?"

Kiana shrugged. She searched for the right thing to say. From the moment she woke up at Genevieve's house, she'd been out of her comfort zone. Hell, since she'd arrived in New Orleans for that matter.

"Just the way you are...so forward and..."

Genevieve nodded. "I see. Big bad stud ain't used to be being asked out on dates, huh? Yeah, you right. I am different." She smiled and stared into Kiana's eyes.

Kiana looked away with a nervous laugh. The man came out of the store with a small bottle wrapped in a paper bag; he cinched it about the neck and slid it inside his jacket. He looked around and jogged up the street.

"I told you it's not that," Kiana said. "I can't really explain it."

"Meet me tomorrow at noon. Give yourself a chance to figure it out," Genevieve said.

"Okay," Kiana said. "I'll meet you in the lobby. Noon."

Genevieve grinned. Kiana thanked her again then turned to head inside the hotel. She stopped at the revolving glass door and watched Genevieve turn the bike around and hop on. She found a break between staggered groups of pedestrians and zipped into the street. Kiana waited until she cleared the corner before heading to the liquor store.

## CHAPTER FIVE

*Monday*

Kiana sipped her beer slowly. She glanced at the clock hanging above the cash register. The bartender looked in her direction and she smiled. He smiled back and went back to watching television. The hotel bar, empty save Kiana and an older woman sipping a glass of Zinfandel, was elegantly decorated in black and gray; a brilliant, eclectic blue made appearances as accents in the carpet, couches, and centerpieces in the dining area. Kiana's phone vibrated against the surface of the bar, where it sat face down. She flipped the phone over but didn't answer it. Karyn's name and work number flashed on the screen. Kiana had called her earlier in the morning and left a short message about arriving in New Orleans safely and, of course, being sorry. She knew Karyn would be calling back, but she let the call go to voice mail. She took a long swallow of her lukewarm Heineken and glanced up at the clock. Her phone rang again. Karyn again, but from her cell phone. Kiana picked up her phone and answered it.

"Kiana?" Karyn said, her voice frantic and high-pitched.

"Yes," Kiana said.

"What's going on? I got your messages. New Orleans? Are you serious? What the hell are you thinking? Come home. Today. You need to come home TODAY. I'll get your ticket. And—"

"I can't do that," Kiana said, interrupting Karyn's string of desperate questions and urgent directives.

Papers ruffled in the background, and Kiana heard phones ringing, keyboards clicking. Kiana could see Karyn clear as day, her hair pulled into a neat ponytail at the base of her neck, simple button-up blouse, and light colored skirt suit. Karyn's job, account something or another—Kiana could never remember her title—meant decent money but monotony, stability but stagnation.

Karyn lowered her voice. "Yes, you can," she whispered into the phone.

"No, I can't," Kiana said. She looked at the clock again. "I haven't spoken to Michelle yet. Not for real."

"You don't need to speak to her."

"But I do, Karyn," she said. "I have to know if—"

"All you need to know, you already know," Karyn said, cutting Kiana off. She exhaled heavily into the receiver. "Come home, Kiana."

"Just give me a couple days. All I need is a couple days."

"Look, I have to go," Karyn whispered. "I'm going to call you when I get off." She cleared her throat against the sound of keystrokes. "Answer your phone when I do."

"I will," Kiana said. She made eye contact with the bartender.

"I mean it, Kiana. Answer your damn phone."

"I will," she said. "I promise."

Karyn hung up in a hurry. Kiana placed her phone on the bar. She stared at her reflection in the mirrored wall behind the bar. The New Orleans humidity frizzed the ends of her thick, kinky hair, creating a halo of dark coils and curls around her head. She looked tired, her eyes dull and strained, but she had no bags or dark circles underneath them. She shook her head. She needed a jolt, something to shake her senses.

"Can I get shot of Maker's?" she said when the bartender finally made his way over to her.

The bartender poured her up and asked her if she wanted another beer. Kiana shook her head. She slammed the shot then chased it with the last of her beer.

"Just charge it all to my room," she said. "Four thirty-eight." She slid off the barstool, grabbed her phone, and pulled her small tin of Altoids from her front pocket. She popped one mint, crunched it, and inhaled through the tingling coolness. She placed a second mint on her tongue and rolled it around in her mouth as she walked toward the couches across from the check-in counters.

Genevieve walked through the glass doors of the hotel and into the lobby at exactly 11:59. She looked cool and comfortable in short khaki shorts and white tank top, her small messenger bag across her shoulder. She waved at Kiana and smiled. Although Genevieve hadn't hinted toward what they were going to do, it seemed Kiana had the right idea with her jeans and orange T-shirt. She walked to meet Genevieve in the middle of the lobby.

"Ready?" Genevieve asked.

Kiana crunched up the last of her Altoid. "Yeah. Let's go." She slid her phone into her back pocket along with her wallet, her flask filling the opposite pocket. She pushed the small flask down instinctively, hoping the silver twist cap wasn't protruding too much.

Instead of a bike ride, Genevieve and Kiana rode the streetcar through the city, talking about New Orleans architecture and culture. Genevieve told Kiana stories about growing up in the city and how hard it was to leave when she went to college in North Carolina. She talked about Katrina, her voice cracking when she described watching the horror on the news and not being able to do anything about it.

"I 'bout fell out when my grandmother finally called to say she was all right," Genevieve said, her eyes watering. "She made it through the hurricane just to have a stroke a year later. I found her. In the kitchen of our old house, on the floor. Rushed her to the hospital and they tried, but she just wouldn't wake back up." She wiped her eyes.

"I'm sorry," Kiana said, pushing down memories of her mother. They bubbled up like acid in the back of her throat. She swallowed. "I'm really sorry."

"No, I'm sorry." Genevieve gave a wry laugh. "Being a downer." She looked out the window then reached up to yank the cord for the next stop. "Come on," she said, grabbing Kiana's hand.

They exited the streetcar and walked across the street and up the block. They stopped at the wide entrance to Oak Grove Cemetery.

"So, about being a downer…" Kiana said. She looked at Genevieve, who curled her lightly-glossed lips into a grin. The sunlight caught her eyes just right, flecks of gold twinkled in the soft brown, and Kiana felt herself smiling too.

"I know, I know," Genevieve said. "To be honest, our trip is part errand, part sight-seeing. I usually go visit Nana, my grandmother, every Sunday, but yesterday, I had an unexpected guest." She smiled. "So, I'm thinking I can show you the mysterious wonder of a N'Awlins cemetery and get my weekly visit in. We can leave here and go to the more famous ones, see Marie Laveau and Homer Plessy. Then, we can head to Jackson

Square to get you a beignet. We'll do all the touristy things. What you say to that?"

"I'm not really here as a tourist," Kiana said then stopped. She was there on a mission. A love mission that she was failing miserably. It didn't feel right to tell Genevieve the truth though. She seemed nice, and Kiana liked her energy. The shot of Maker's and beer had warmed her nicely, and without a real plan to deal with Michelle, she figured she'd let it ride. No sense spoiling a good afternoon. She shrugged. "I mean, not officially."

"Yeah, you right. But, baby, you can't come to N'Awlins and not check out at least one cemetery," Genevieve said.

Kiana looked across the busy street. A streetcar headed in the opposite direction slowed to a stop. "Well, let's go. I am curious about the graves. We bury folks deep in the ground where I come from." She held her arm for Genevieve to take. They linked arms and walked through the wrought iron gates.

Even in the daylight, it was spooky. The graves, old and waist level, made Kiana uneasy. Something about the dead being on the same ground with her, on the earth instead of inside it, on top rather than below, made her question her existence, made her feel in-between.

"See those ferns?" Genevieve said, pointing a long, slender finger at the leafy plants growing along the crooked, low branches and thick, lined trunks of the oak trees standing guard between the crypts. "They're called resurrection ferns. They live for a long time, even when there ain't any water."

"How can a plant survive without water?" Kiana asked. She stepped to a fern trail that ran down the side of a tree they passed. She touched the pale, leathery fronds, plucking one of the oblong leaves.

"When there ain't no water, it curls up and turns brown just like that. Looks just like it deaded right on the tree. Then, when the rain comes, it unfurls, green and full. Resurrected. Alive again."

Kiana looked back at the ferns as they continued walking. There was more life than she expected in the cemetery. Plants with tiny white blossoms peeked out from cracks in the tombs and hung down from the eaves of crypts. Vines wound around statues and columns. Rocks crunched underneath their feet, patches of thick, wide-bladed grass surrounded the graves and spotted the paths. Genevieve came to a stop in front of a long, rectangular cement grave flanked by two large tombs separated by a rusted iron gate. She stood in silence.

"So this is where your grandmother is buried?" Kiana asked the unnecessary question just to hear her own voice.

"Yes," Genevieve said. "She rests here." Genevieve took Kiana's hand and led her around the side of the grave. She knelt beside her grandmother's resting place, and Kiana swallowed hard, looking around.

She read the names on the nearby crypts, noticing the water lines that ran around the length and width of them. Some graves were marked with just last names in hard, serious fonts. Herbert, Bordelon, Pedarre. Others had names and sayings, "No work began in life shall pause for death," and, "I pass but shall not die." Kiana shuddered. She wandered around to get a closer look at the tomb to the right of Genevieve's grandmother. The large, wide stone structure boasted a crest crossed with two swords with a flame in the center but no names. Off to the side and pushed back, Kiana found a winged woman, on a pedestal and at least six feet tall, crafted in cracked and stained stone. Wings unfurled behind her, she held her hands out in supplication. The base of the statue held several names, all of them with dates that ranged between two and five years apart; the last name in the list didn't even span that. The last addition, Angelique Devereux, marked a life that lasted only seven days.

A chill ran through Kiana, goose bumps instantly covering her shoulders and arms. Her phone vibrated in her back pocket. She thought of her flask, a libation for the week-old baby, a slow burn of whiskey to still her heart. She swallowed hard and walked back over to Genevieve.

Genevieve had moved to the opposite side of her grand-mother's grave. Dried splotches of wax and melted down stumps of red and white candles sat in clumps near crinkled flower petals and sunken in fruit. Kiana looked away from the side of the grave and stepped around to the front. She read the name displayed on the iron plate, stained green with age and water damage, at the foot of the crypt.

"Emeline Durand," Kiana whispered.

Genevieve nodded. "That's my Nana."

There were two other names: Bernard Durand and Xavier Durand.

"Her brothers are buried there, too. My uncles," Genevieve said. "I didn't know them very well, can barely remember them, but my Nana talked about them all the time."

"The years aren't listed," Kiana said, pointing at the plate then quickly lowering her hand. It felt wrong to point.

"Nope," Genevieve said. "She didn't want them listed. She just wanted this." She grabbed Kiana's hand and gently tugged her back over to the side of the tomb. She nodded toward the stumps of spent candles at the base of the stone grave. Nearly hidden by the wax were the words: I AM NOT GONE.

Kiana stiffened. She shivered and rubbed at her arms. Genevieve noticed Kiana shifting and looking around.

"You all right?" she asked. "You want to go?"

Kiana did want to leave. She was spooked, but embarrassed. She wished she'd had two shots of whiskey instead of one. She might've been less affected, more numb to it all.

"No," she said. "I'm fine." She yanked nervously at the bottom of her shirt. She remembered a gold necklace Karyn had given her when she turned eleven. It was a cross, thin and delicate with a cubic zirconium in the center. She hadn't thought of it in years, but suddenly she wished she had it. She clutched at the neck of her T-shirt. She wished she had kept the necklace, wondered where it was. It had been her mother's, the only thing of hers left. Karyn had given it to her as a way to remember. Kiana bit the inside of her cheek and finger-picked the back of her afro. She didn't want to think of her mother. She didn't want to think of anything. Fidgety and restless, she slid her hand toward her back pocket, touching the top of her flask with her fingertips. Her phone vibrated again, and it made her jump.

"You sure you all right?" Genevieve asked.

"Yes," Kiana snapped. "Stop asking me that."

"Okay. We'll go soon, all right? I have to do something first." She went into the small leather messenger bag she wore and pulled out a small bottle half full of water. Near the headstone of the grave sat a small, water-stained ceramic bowl, the hand-painted flowers on the front faded by the sun. Genevieve poured water from the bottle into the bowl and set the bottle on the grass beside the grave.

Kiana wanted to ask Genevieve what she was doing, but her lips wouldn't move. She felt stuck, everything around her on pause—the light wind, the traffic outside the gates.

"It's like an offering," Genevieve said as if reading her mind. She dug into her bag and took out a small brown pear and a plum so deep purple it looked black. She held the fruit then stepped back from the tomb. "I've officially scared you," she said.

"No," Kiana said. "People put flowers down and…" She frowned. "I guess I've only known people to put down flowers. This is…"

"Crazy? Spooky?"

"Different," Kiana said. "Definitely different. You're definitely different. And…" She took a deep breath and exhaled slowly, looking away because her eyes stung with tears and she didn't want Genevieve to see. She read the words along the bottom of the tomb, moving her lips but not making a sound. *I am not gone.*

"And what?" Genevieve asked, stretching to place the fruit atop the crypt, as far away from the edge as possible. She exhaled and stepped closer to Kiana. "And what?"

"And it makes me want to be different," Kiana said softly. She glanced at her feet; her face flushed with heat, her eyes still burning.

"Baby," Genevieve said. "You seem just fine to me."

Kiana forced a smile that she hoped didn't look too awkward. Her lips trembled. "Can we leave now?"

"Yeah. We can go." Genevieve frowned, her lips a straight line of concern. "We'll go to Jackson Square and—"

"I actually just want to go back to the hotel," Kiana interrupted. "I've got some phone calls to return, and I should probably see what's going on with the wedding stuff."

Genevieve nodded. "You don't have to explain," she said. She grabbed Kiana's arm. "Let's go."

When they arrived back at the hotel, Kiana damn near ran to the bar. She caught herself and turned to Genevieve.

"Thank you for today," she said.

"My pleasure," Genevieve said. She adjusted her bag. "I hope I didn't…"

"No, you didn't," Kiana said.

"Why don't you come over for dinner?" Genevieve said. "Baby, you haven't lived until you've tasted my gumbo."

Kiana looked over her shoulder to the hotel restaurant and bar. She sighed and reached around to her back pocket, then pulled out her phone. She glanced down at it, swiping the screen to display several missed calls and pending voice and text messages. Just looking at the alerts made her head ache.

Genevieve nodded. She stuffed her hands in the pockets of her shorts. "Okay. Right. I don't mean to keep you."

"No," Kiana said. "I mean, I do have a couple things to do, but dinner sounds nice." She smiled. Spending time with Genevieve meant ignoring more calls, avoiding the inevitable conversation with Karyn, and stalling another confrontation with Michelle. It also meant spending more time with Genevieve, which was refreshing and challenging in a way Kiana hadn't felt in a long while. As much as it was counterproductive, it was attractive and exciting. "Let's do it," she said.

"Great," Genevieve said. She took her phone out of her bag and they exchanged numbers.

"I'll text you my address," Genevieve said, "and you can come by around…nine?"

"Perfect." Kiana grinned. "I'll see you later. I can't wait."

Genevieve blushed and spun on her heels. Kiana, unable to resist, watched her tight ass and long legs as she walked toward the glass doors. Genevieve looked over her shoulder and waved at Kiana before pushing herself through the revolving door.

Kiana shook her head and exhaled loudly. Instead of heading to the bar, she walked to the elevators. She scrolled through her missed calls while in the elevator. Two total from Karyn, five from Michelle, and one from her manager at New Horizons. She stuffed her phone into her pocket and pulled out her flask. She drained it before the elevator dinged, signaling her floor.

❖

Showered and dressed in jeans and a simple blue button up, which she wore open over a white tank top, Kiana made her way down to the lobby. While in the elevator, she listened to her messages while absent-mindedly yanking at random locks of her thick, unruly hair. Her manager, his voice nasally and flat, announced that a "no call, no show" was grounds for dismissal. She needed to call him as soon as possible if she had any intentions of keeping her job. Karyn, frustrated and angry at another broken promise, left long messages where she alternately begged Kiana to come home and cursed her out, finally asking at the end of the second message: "When will you get tired of lying?" Michelle's messages were short: "Call me," "Tell me where you're staying," and "I need to see you." The last message, the need, made Kiana's breath catch, a tightness in her throat and flutter in the lowest part of her stomach. She stepped out of the elevator and eyed the bar. Shaking her head against the urge to stop for a drink, she walked out to the street to hail a cab. When one pulled up, she stepped toward it then stopped. She waved her hand and smiled, sending the car away. She walked up the street to the liquor store and picked up two bottles of wine. A red and a white. She wasn't sure which went best with gumbo.

When she arrived at Genevieve's place, she turned her phone off. She knocked on the door, nervous and hesitant. A barefooted Genevieve opened the door dressed in a black tank top and leggings that matched the deep red polish on her toes. She smiled; a white apron was cinched around her waist and splotched with brownish-red sauce and faded yellow stains.

"I didn't picture you for the apron type," Kiana said as she stepped into the small carriage house. She narrowed her eyes and added a playful frown as she tried to figure out exactly what she meant. She hadn't really pictured Genevieve at all. She pushed through the fog of her memory and recalled Genevieve's casual sexiness as she leaned against the doorway the first morning they met. She was thin and graceful, but not at all delicate. Her strength was obvious in her voice, the husky lilt in her rolling sentences, the confident, sexy laugh that chased away shadows.

Genevieve did a slight curtsy. "My gumbo is serious business. Besides, I said I was cooking for you, so I wanted to dress the part." She closed the door behind Kiana and walked into the kitchen.

"It smells amazing in here." Kiana grinned. She held up the two bottles of wine, one in each hand. "Red or white?"

Genevieve stood at the counter slicing a half loaf of warm, crusty bread. "Whichever you prefer." She spun around, went into a cabinet above the counter, and retrieved a stemless wine glass. She placed it on the breakfast bar then went into a drawer for the wine key. She placed it next to the glass.

"One glass?"

Genevieve nodded. "I'm not having any," she said.

Kiana scrunched her eyebrows. "Wait a minute." She bit her lip and narrowed her eyes at Genevieve as she grabbed the wine key. "Why not?" she challenged.

Genevieve took a deep breath. "I don't drink." She shrugged and placed the pieces of bread in a small wooden bowl. "And after the other night, I don't suppose you need to go too hard yourself."

Kiana scoffed then went silent, concentrating on opening the Merlot. She screwed the wine key into the bottle and yanked up. The soft, wet pop of the cork broke the silence between them. Kiana poured herself a large glass of wine. She stared into the wine, the light from the kitchen casting through the liquid, making it look like blood. She looked into Genevieve's eyes as she drank from the glass. She took two sips.

"You don't drink ever?" Kiana asked. She drank from her wine glass.

"Nope," Genevieve said. She turned from Kiana and picked up a large spoon to stir the bubbling contents of the tall, stainless pot atop the stove.

Kiana shook her head. "Why not?"

Genevieve didn't answer. She scooped up a little gumbo into the spoon and held her hand under it. She stepped toward Kiana, blowing at the small bit of stew on the spoon. She leaned over the breakfast bar.

"Taste," she said.

Kiana leaned in slowly, parting her lips. She sucked at the gumbo in the spoon and swallowed. Her eyes widened.

"Oh my God," she said, a slow, sweet heat teasing her taste buds. Celery, bell peppers, okra, and onions asserted themselves against the full flavors of fresh shrimp, savory chicken, and spicy sausage. She licked her lips. "That's delicious!"

Genevieve smiled and returned to the stove. She went about the kitchen grabbing bowls and spoons. She gestured toward the futon in the front room. "We'll eat in there," she said.

Kiana turned and noticed the two placemats on the table in front of the futon. She took the bottle and her wine glass over to the table and settled on the futon. Genevieve placed the bowl of bread on the table then returned with a steaming serving of gumbo for Kiana, who waited until Genevieve returned with her own bowl before leaning in to take a piece of bread.

They ate in an awkward silence at first. Kiana's mind raced in circles. The text and voice mail messages from Michelle, the things she wanted to say, what she planned to do. She looked at Genevieve and smiled; she didn't want to think about those things. All she wanted was to enjoy the delicious meal in front of her and the beautiful woman beside her. She drank from her wine and closed her eyes.

"Do you like it?" Genevieve asked.

"Yeah. I love it," Kiana said. She smiled. She returned her wine to the table and slurped another mouthful of gumbo.

"It's my nana's recipe. She used to make it every week. She'd usually start it Friday night. I'd help her chop up the vegetables, peel and devein the shrimp, mix the roux. She'd sing to me and—"

"So why don't you drink?" Kiana interrupted as she refilled her glass. She had been drinking steadily since she sat down, taking a sip or two between bites of food.

Genevieve cleared her throat. "I used to. I used to drink quite a bit. I had a tough time when my nana passed. She raised me. I never knew my father or my mother. Her family was small, too. Her two younger brothers passed on before her."

Kiana wanted to say something, something comforting and certain. She drank instead, knowing that her words always came out too casual or too careless.

Genevieve continued. "Sometimes it all seems very sad, then other times it seems like she was destined to survive all that dark family history, like she was meant to be a light for me." She shifted in her seat. "Anyway, she was all I had, and when I lost her, I came apart."

Kiana took another drink of her wine. She held the tart liquid in her mouth for a moment before she swallowed.

Genevieve shook her head. "I felt guilty enough leaving her to go to college. Then, when Katrina hit and I hadn't lost her, I guess I relaxed a little. I felt like maybe she was right."

"Right about what?" Kiana said, leaning in.

"Nana used to say that she was going to live forever," Genevieve said with sigh. Her mouth curved into a crooked grin. "She said that I was her life's work. That her job was to see me healthy and happy, loving and being loved. She would kiss me here, here, and here"—Genevieve tapped her each side of her face and her forehead as she spoke—"then say 'no work begun in life shall stop for death.'"

"I saw that on a grave today," Kiana said.

"Is that right?"

"Yeah," Kiana said. She took a deep breath and drank from her wine glass. She put the glass down and shivered slightly.

"What's wrong?" Genevieve looked into Kiana's eyes with concern.

"Nothing," Kiana said, looking away. The soulful light in Genevieve's eyes invited Kiana to come closer, called her in from the cold darkness of her own painful memories in such an easy, obvious way that it caught her off guard. It was too much. "It's just...I keep trying to get comfortable with you. And I can't. You make me think about things I don't want to think about. Things that I push away, things that I..."

"Try to drown with drinks," Genevieve said.

Kiana turned to her with a frown. "That kind of shit right there. That's..." She grabbed her drink from the table, the wine sloshing around the bowl of the glass. She drank, tilting her head back. She refilled her glass, emptying the bottle.

"I'm sorry, Kiana," Genevieve said. "It's just that there's something about you that I really like, and I know we just met, but..."

"You don't even fucking know me," Kiana said. She held the wine glass, rolling the wine around, watching the legs drip down and the red wine swirl. She drank. She looked at Genevieve out of the corner of her eye, unable to resist watching her as she furrowed her brows in thought and concern. Kiana wanted to make a move, a kiss or a touch, something to move from the emotional to the physical, but she felt stuck. She needed something easy, something like a balm for the stinging mess that was her insides, but being around Genevieve challenged her to go deeper than topical relief; she felt like Genevieve was offering her a healing. She wasn't sure she really wanted to be healed, didn't even know if it would work.

"You don't know me, Genevieve," she repeated, hating that she was even thinking so deeply about it. Kiana stared at the blood red wine in her glass.

"I'm trying to get to know you," Genevieve said. "But, baby, you making that shit hard." She leaned back from her food, turning to face Kiana. She folded one of her legs under the other and rested her arm across the back of the futon. "Tell me something," she said. "Tell me something about you. Something that matters."

Kiana cut her eyes at Genevieve, sizing her up. Fuck it, she said to herself. She drank from her glass, nearly draining it. She set it on the table then leaned back, matching Genevieve's position, but resting her hands in her lap.

"In the cemetery today, I thought about this necklace my sister gave me. It was my mother's. I hadn't thought about it in years. Shit, I haven't thought about *her* in years. On the bike, I had a flashback, a real memory. I don't get them often. Real memories." Kiana swallowed hard and stared down at her hands. "My mother died when I was five."

"I'm so sorry," Genevieve said. She crinkled her eyebrows, her lips a straight line.

"I have exactly two memories of her, neither of them involve her face. I never see her face," Kiana said. She closed her eyes and saw only her mother's back. The slopes of shoulders, the curls of hair at the nape of her neck, the alert, protective way she moved her head from side to side as she pedaled around the neighborhood, her baby daughter in tow. Kiana squeezed her eyes tighter, remembering the wrinkles of loose skin at her mother's elbow, the jutting sharpness of her shoulder blades, and the flop of her small, bare feet as she jerked and shook on the living room floor. Kiana opened her eyes. "I can only see her from behind. Her lying on the floor. My sister shoving me away, pushing me away." Kiana's voice caught, her eyes filling with tears and bottom lip trembling. She hated crying. She wiped at her eyes and cleared her throat, fighting it.

Genevieve placed a hand on Kiana's thigh.

"It's just me and my sister," Kiana said. Always a sucker for touch, she looked down at Genevieve's hand and a wave of heat pulsed through her. She took a deep breath. "It's always just been me and my sister."

"Where is she? Your sister, I mean."

"Back home. In Chicago." Kiana shrugged. She wanted to stop talking. She needed to stop talking. If she kept on, she'd be crying. If she started crying, she'd be pathetic and sad, and she didn't want to be pathetic and sad. She glanced at Genevieve, and she was giving her that look that she hated, a look that said, "I'm sorry for you." She didn't want anyone to be sorry for her. She glanced at Genevieve's hand, searching for an escape from the depth of the moment. The long fingers and short, neat, glossy nails. Kiana thought of Genevieve's capable hands as she prepared their food, wondered if the spicy seasonings and rich flavors clung to her fingers, if the gumbo would come alive against her tongue in the same way if she sucked Genevieve's fingertips. Kiana's body responded to the musings, heat building between her legs and desire moistening her mouth. She reached over to the table and picked up her wine. She sipped and concentrated on the tart bite of it on her tongue, the sharp, full taste as she swallowed.

"So your sister raised you?" Genevieve asked. She returned her hand to her lap, and Kiana wondered if she were doing her mind reading tricks again.

"See," she said. Kiana drank from the wine, looking at Genevieve over the rim of the glass. She finished the wine and put the empty glass on the table next to the empty bottle. "This is what I'm talking about. I don't want to talk about this." She scooted forward. Genevieve didn't move.

"Baby, I just asked you to tell me something about you," Genevieve said. "You chose what you told me." She raised her eyebrow. "Maybe you do want to talk about it, but you don't know you want to talk about it. It's trying to get out and breathe, but you keep stuffing it back in. You can't force it down forever."

Kiana shook her head. "Do you always talk like that?" She felt her wine; it danced a waltz across her skin.

"Like what?" Genevieve shrugged.

"Like that," Kiana said, inching closer. "Like a poem. You talk like you're reciting a fucking poem." She giggled. "You can't force it, baby. It must breathe," she said mocking Genevieve. She moved closer and licked her lips.

Genevieve narrowed her eyes and moved her arm from the back of the futon. She crossed her arms over her chest. "That's how I sound?"

"Yeah," Kiana said. "I like it though. It's sexy. And the way you say 'baby' like you've loved me my whole life. I noticed it since I been here. Everybody says it. Is that a New Orleans thing? The way you say it though…that shit is hot. Say something else." She moved closer to Genevieve. She could smell her, the earthy scent of dirt, the faint sweetness of ripe fruit, and the savory saltiness of the gumbo.

"I've spoken enough for today," Genevieve said. "You're the one with things to say. You're the one with feelings threatening to dead you right where you sit."

"Mmmmm," Kiana said. She closed all those feelings off, all that painful memory and conversation. She knew how to make herself feel better. She needed release. The wine fueled her as she leaned forward, aiming to touch her lips to Genevieve's lips. She closed her eyes and anticipated the feeling: soft, warm, wet.

Genevieve moved back, holding her arms up and placing her hands on Kiana's shoulders, stopping her.

Kiana opened her eyes. "Come on…" she said, her voice a gentle whisper.

"You're drunk," Genevieve said.

"I'm not," Kiana countered.

Genevieve pushed herself up from the futon and began clearing the table. Kiana, rejected and angry, watched her as she moved about in the kitchen. She grabbed at the wine bottle and shook it over her glass. A single drop plopped into the bottom of her glass. She lifted the glass and drank it, the spot of wine so small, she couldn't taste it or feel it against her tongue. Genevieve shook her head as she came back to the table for Kiana's dish and the bowl of bread.

"You can stay here if you want," Genevieve said. "You can take my bed. I'll sleep out here."

Kiana stood up. "Fuck that," she said. "I'm going back to my hotel."

"You shouldn't," Genevieve said. "You can stay here. It's better. It's safer."

Kiana rolled her eyes. She walked over to the counter and picked up the wine key. She began opening the second bottle of wine.

"Come on, baby," Genevieve said. She placed the dirty dishes on the counter. "You've had enough."

"Don't 'baby' me," Kiana said, "You don't know me. I know me. I know when I've had enough."

Genevieve snatched the corkscrew from Kiana's hands.

"Ouch!" she said.

"Sorry," Genevieve said.

"No, you aren't," Kiana said. She turned on her heels and headed for the door. "I'm calling a cab and going back to my hotel. I don't need this shit." She opened the door and slammed it behind her.

The cool night air felt good against her face. Her cheeks warm with frustration and skin hot with desire, she stood in the garden, looking around at the shadows the plants made. The blossoms closed tight against the darkness and fountain trickling like a lonely, hidden stream. She was mad. She was horny. She was lonely. She took her phone from her back pocket and turned it on as she walked up the narrow path to the street. Once on the sidewalk, she called a cab. While she waited, she called Michelle, who didn't answer. She left a message, a very short one, much like the ones Michelle left for her.

The cab arrived, and she climbed in.

"Holiday Inn on Royal, please," she said. The driver nodded. Before he pulled off, Kiana's phone buzzed with a text message from Michelle. Two words: I can't.

"I changed my mind," Kiana said. "Take me to the Quarter. The far end."

❖

The club Kiana settled on was hot. And dark. The music pulsed, shaking everything, the walls, the floor, the bar, the light fixtures. Everything rattled and buzzed, trembled and quaked. She smelled sweat, smoke, and sex. The packed dance floor contrasted the nearly empty bar. A few people huddled at the far end of the dark lounge area beside the bar, but the chairs lining the bar had long been abandoned for the hot, urgent intimacy of the dance floor. The music amplified the energy of the club all the same. Kiana could feel the bass in her chest, the snap of the snare in her teeth, the crashing keyboards behind her eyes. She sat at the bar, two empty shot glasses in front of her, and a full one on the way.

"Make it two," she yelled over the music to the bare-chested bartender in sparkly red hot pants. He threw her a kiss over his shoulder and grabbed another shot glass from the shelf overhead. A woman in a black and white dress stepped to the bar, leaning on the back of the empty chair rather than sitting in it. Her dress, a perfect fit against her hips and thighs, barely covered the curve of her ass as she pressed herself forward on the bar.

"Have a drink with me," Kiana said, eyeing her fishnet stockings, accented with double-stitched diamond shapes. She cleared her throat and said it again. Bold, fearless, and certain. "Have a drink with me."

The woman turned. She smiled at Kiana over her shoulder. "Why should I?"

"Because if you don't, I'll be drinking alone," Kiana said. "And you know what they say about drinking alone." She frowned and shook her head. "Very, very bad."

The woman, her round olive-skinned face open, kind, and framed by straight black hair in an asymmetrical bob, pursed her lips. She nodded toward Kiana's empty shot glasses. "Looks like you've already been drinking alone," she said.

Kiana glanced at the glasses and scrunched her eyebrows. She turned back to the woman. "You're right. I have been."

"So, why don't you keep going?" The woman shrugged. She cut her eyes; heavily lined with mascara, cat-like and smoky, they challenged Kiana to continue.

"I'm trying to change my wicked ways," she said.

The woman looked Kiana up and down. She turned her body completely, no longer leaning on the bar, but sliding into the space between the empty chair and where Kiana sat. She licked her lips. "That's too bad," she said.

The bartender set the two shots down in front of them. He winked at Kiana and raised his eyebrows at the woman.

Kiana slid the shot toward the woman and lifted her own. "Cheers?"

The woman picked up the shot and raised it toward Kiana's. She stopped. "Wait. You ordered this before you asked me if I wanted it?"

"Yeah. So?" Kiana grinned, inhaling the woman's scent: cloves, lime, and tequila.

"That's awfully cocky, don't you think?" the woman said.

"No, no," Kiana said. "Not cocky. Confident. There's a very important difference."

"What's the difference?"

"I'll tell you in the morning," Kiana said. She tapped her shot against the woman's glass then touched it to the bar.

"Now you're being cocky," the woman said, lifting her shot and laughing.

They slammed the shots back.

"You ain't seen nothing yet," Kiana said. She lifted her hand for the bartender. "Two more, buddy," she said.

❖

The woman was lava. Molten, hot lava. She moved over Kiana's skin slow and steady, thick and rolling, heavy, hot, and destructive. Her name unimportant, her body a volcano, Kiana's fingers dove deep inside her, finding a fiery rage churning and roiling around her knuckles. She shook from the inside, trembling and coming apart. "I don't even know your name," the woman had said before Kiana kissed her in the elevator and, "I told myself I'd stop doing this," she had whispered into Kiana's neck as clothes loosened and fell to the floor. Her doubts and hesitations, better judgment and healthy caution, everything hard and jagged about her, everything solid and certain crumbled and splashed into the pool of fire between them as they rolled and rumbled across the bed. The woman's liquid heat coated Kiana's fingers, their sweat sizzling on their skin. Finally, the eruption. The rush, the spray. It caught Kiana off guard. She removed her hand and looked down at the woman. All she could see was light, the lamp, the sun, the moon, the streetlight, she didn't know which, but it glimmered off the woman's face, making it glowing brass, the length of her slender nose and perfection of pouty lips. She dipped down to kiss her. The woman turned her face and flipped over, situating herself on top of Kiana.

The light hid her features, a blur of movement and warmth, the woman's mouth seemed everywhere at once. She went down; Kiana felt lips and tongue and teeth. She opened her legs in invitation, and the woman accepted. Kiana looked down at the top of the woman's head. She couldn't remember her name or if she'd even asked what it was. She couldn't remember the woman's face. She recalled only light, glowing, comforting light, and heat. Light and heat. She smiled and arched her body up, offering herself to the sun, fucking the sun.

It was these moments, these times of complete abandon that Kiana felt most secure. An oxymoron. Uncertain and exposed, she let go of everything and became sure and protected. She rode the rising heat between her legs, her body curling with uncontrollable sensation. She called out to God, claiming and clutching at something bigger than herself.

"Oh my God!" Kiana screamed. The woman moaned.

The heat waned only to return again, building up, threatening to explode again. She shuddered against the woman's mouth. Everything she knew and didn't know swallowed by flames, extinguished against the surface of the sun. This was Kiana's salvation. Her second coming. She threw it all into the sky as she thrust her hips up—Michelle, Genevieve, Karyn, her mother, gumbo and wine, bikes and bread, bass thumps and shots of whiskey—and it burned away to nothing, only pleasure remained. And she called out to God when she came again. The woman joined her in the bucking climax, the bed thumping against the wall. If only she could have this, the pleasure of coming together with another in a single moment suspended in time. There were no expectations in that moment. There were no disappointments. There were no memories. There was only now, now, now, and now again. Kiana closed her eyes with a wish that now could be all there was, that now could be forever, and that forever could be release. No pent-up pressure of the past, no festering fantasies for the future. Just the numbing, nourishing now.

She collapsed against the bed. A blur of light as the woman rose up from between her thighs. Then darkness.

## CHAPTER SIX

*Tuesday*

Kiana slid out of bed, careful not to wake the stranger who lay beside her. She walked on her toes to the bathroom, stepping over the pile of clothes near the foot of the bed. Once inside, she washed her face with splashes of cold water. She looked at herself in the mirror. Her lips and eyes were puffy, her hair matted on one side. A fog of drunkenness lingered, her thoughts muddled and slow. She sat on the toilet and closed her eyes, trying to remember how her night with Genevieve ended, what led her to the club, and where the curvy woman with jet-black hair who moaned and moved about in the bed came from. Patches of memory—bass thumps and shots, a packed dance floor and a pair of sparkly hot pants—revealed little. She opened her eyes with a deep sigh then glanced over her shoulder at the abandoned cocktail that sat on the edge of the sink. She grabbed it, sniffed it, and swallowed it down. The stale, muted bittersweet of watered down whiskey managed to give her a bit of a jolt. She shrugged and stood to wash her hands and face.

"Kiana," the woman called from beyond the bathroom door. "Kiana."

Kiana winced as she toweled her face. She didn't know the woman's name. She wracked her brain. Cat-eyes. Asymmetric bob. Full, pouty lips. All face, no name. She opened the bathroom door and stood in the doorway.

"Yes?" she said.

"Come back to bed," the woman said. "It's too early, and I'm not done with you yet."

Kiana smiled. She walked toward the bed. "I'm sorry," she said. "I've actually got a lot to do today, so…" She stopped at the foot of the bed. The woman sat up, the crumpled sheet fell from the point of her breasts. Her nipples, pale pink against her light skin, stood erect. She crawled toward Kiana.

"That's not what I want to hear," the woman said. She stopped on all fours, directly in front of Kiana. She looked up at her, eyes strangely alert.

Kiana took a step away from the bed. Her phone rang. She dashed to the side of the bed and grabbed it. She looked at the screen and slid the button to answer the call.

"Hey, Karyn!" Kiana smiled and walked toward the windows. She moved her face away from the phone and whispered to the disappointed woman in her bed. "I've got to take this." The woman frowned.

Kiana found her jeans on the floor and pulled them on, cradling the phone between her face and shoulder. "Now before you start, I know I was supposed to answer your call. I know we need to talk and straighten things out. We can do that now. We can settle everything today." She made a helpless face and shrugged toward the woman again. She seemed to finally take the hint and stomped her way from the bed to the bathroom. Kiana waited until she heard the water splashing against the sink before she continued.

"I know, Karyn," she said. "I'm a dickhead." Karyn went in, cursing and yelling into the phone. Kiana rolled her eyes. She'd heard it all before: selfish, brat, stupid, liar, promises, nothing, careless, rude, weak, impulsive, drunk, unclear, impatient, and oblivious. "Karyn, I'm sorry."

The woman came out the bathroom and collected her dress and shoes. She slipped her dress over her head, ran her fingers through her hair, and tugged on her shoes.

"We can talk about all of it," Kiana said into the phone. "I promise."

The woman twisted her lips and walked over to Kiana. She kissed her on the cheek opposite the phone, her hand trailing its way between Kiana's breasts and down to the unfastened V of her jeans. She slipped a hand inside. Kiana bit her lip. Karyn droned on. The woman expertly found Kiana's clit and rubbed it. Kiana grabbed the woman's wrist and held it, stopping the delicious rhythm of her slender fingers. The woman smirked and slid her hand out of Kiana's pants and shook her head with a sly grin.

"I left my number," the woman said. She turned and left.

Kiana sighed into the phone while Karyn continued, rattling off flight times and reasons she needed to come home: job, responsibility, and moving on. Kiana walked over to the nightstand. The woman had scrawled her number on the notepad next to the phone. She picked it up and read the number. Just her number, no name.

"No, I hear everything you're saying," Kiana said. She ran a thumb over the number and tossed the pad back onto the table. "Karyn, I really just got up. Let me call you back. I promise I'll call you back." After a short silence, Karyn just hung up. Kiana blew out a loud breath. She placed her phone on the nightstand and sat on the edge of the bed. She stared at her cell phone, debating calling Karyn back. Just as she reached for it, the hotel phone rang. She eyed it suspiciously before picking it up on the third ring.

"Hello?"

It was Genevieve. She said she was downstairs in the lobby.

"I want to take you somewhere so we can talk," she said. "Wear comfortable shoes."

❖

Kiana and Genevieve walked up the street in silence. Kiana wanted to say something, but didn't know where to begin. With no clear memory of just how things ended with them the night before, she didn't know if she needed to apologize or not, demand an apology or not. She usually erred on the side of her own transgression.

"I'm sorry about last night," Genevieve said.

Kiana slowed her pace. "I was about to apologize to you," she said.

"No," Genevieve said. "I'm the one who went too far. It was obvious you didn't want to talk about your mother, and I pushed."

Kiana nodded. She cleared her throat. "Well, I didn't have to get drunk. You made a nice dinner and I…"

"I also don't need to impose my own challenges on you," Genevieve said. "You're a big girl and have been taking care of yourself long before I came along. So, I'm sorry."

Kiana looked at Genevieve, her long, orange maxi dress hugging her small hips as the wind blew. Her eyes, bright and clear, seemed to see into Kiana's very heart. She smiled.

"Apology accepted," Kiana said. They continued across the street and came up on the Riverwalk. Small groups of people walked beneath the large sign welcoming visitors to the Mississippi River. Kiana and Genevieve made their way to the cement path, walking side-by-side. Kiana looked over her shoulder; the wide Mississippi was brown and calm, a slight tint of blue from the sky reflecting against the rippling surface of the water. Long bulk carriers moved slowly in the distance, the hulls a collection of faded two-tones, orange and white, green and black, blue and red. Genevieve stopped and placed a hand on Kiana's back, urging her across the small patch of grass and closer to the rocky shore where carefully placed boulders met the river's edge. They stepped onto a couple of the larger rocks, finding a place to sit beside each other. They looked out at the water, the ships in the distance, and the modest Gretna skyline across the river.

"It's not like I imagined it would be," Kiana said. "The river, I mean."

"No? What did you expect?" Genevieve said.

"I don't know. Busy? Ships everywhere, boxes of cargo in nets swinging, people yelling and pointing and running around blowing whistles." Kiana shrugged.

Genevieve laughed. "You watch too many movies. Old movies." She bumped against Kiana. "It's busy at the port and maybe down by the mall, but we're at the park. It's a different feel around here, baby."

They watched the water. The sky clear, a few puffs of clouds dotted the horizon; with the mild warmth in the air and the gentle breeze, the scene was peaceful.

"I'm glad you called," Kiana said. She sighed. "I haven't been totally honest about why I'm here."

Genevieve raised an eyebrow but didn't say anything.

"I'm here for a wedding, but...it's my ex-girlfriend's wedding." Kiana tapped her toes against the rock beneath her feet. "I'm here to stop it."

"Oh, I see," Genevieve said. She stared across the water, her voice going low and soft. "I'm sorry to hear that."

"That she's getting married on me?" Kiana said. She looked at Genevieve, but Genevieve didn't look at her.

"No. I'm sorry that that's the reason you're here."

Kiana hadn't expected her to be so honest, though she should have. Genevieve seemed incapable of lying. Everything about her was open, clear, true. Genevieve wouldn't look at her. It was obvious the woman liked her, and it was hard for Kiana not to appreciate the interest. It felt good to be wanted. She didn't want to use Genevieve the way she'd used others before and after Michelle, nameless encounters with women whose desires were used against them in ways they didn't realize until the morning after.

"Genevieve, I'm not trying to play you," Kiana said. "I guess that's why I'm being honest with you. It's just that things are really fucked up for me and they have been for a while now. Since Michelle left. The way we ended was just…" Kiana shook her head. She didn't know how to describe the way they ended. She tried to think back to those last days before she left. Not much came back, but just thinking of Michelle brought back glimpses of happier times—snowball fights and snow angels at three a.m., snowflakes glowing against the streetlights, dancing to the drummers at Bongo Beach then looking out at the water daydreaming about Africa, nursing shots and beers at their neighborhood bar pretending to care about whether or not the Bears will make it to the playoffs.

"Does she know you're here?" Genevieve asked.

"What?" Kiana brought herself grudgingly out of her reverie.

"I said does she know you're here?"

Kiana chuckled. "She invited me. How fucked is that?" she said. "I must be a glutton for punishment or something."

"Yeah, you right," Genevieve said. She finally looked at Kiana. "Apparently, you need to figure some things out. Talk to her. It's obvious you're not over her."

"I don't even know what to say," Kiana said. "I have absolutely no plan."

Genevieve stood. She looked down at Kiana and reached out her hand. "Come with me," she said.

Kiana looked up at Genevieve's hand then up into her eyes. "Where are we going?"

Genevieve smiled. "For a ride."

Kiana chuckled. "Last time you offered me a ride, I ended up on your little green bike hanging on for dear life," she said.

"Yeah, you right," Genevieve said. "It's not a bike this time."

"That's all you're going to tell me?"

"Trust me, baby," Genevieve said. She pushed her hand forward, a playful grin settling on her lips. "I mean you no harm. Maybe I can even help you. You need calm. You need caresses from the wind and kisses from the sun. Come with me."

Kiana smiled and shook her head. "There you go talking in stanzas again." She reached up and took Genevieve's hand.

They strolled the length of the Riverwalk, their silences dotted with small chitchat about the city's rich history. Genevieve told Kiana the story of Mardi Gras, the slow, muddy river beside them all the while.

"So basically, it's just wildin' out before starting Lent?" Kiana shrugged. "Then you spend the next month depriving yourself of the things that make you happiest. That's kind of sadistic isn't it? Suffering through withdrawal and deprivation for what? It's not like you win anything for making it through those days. And then you go right back to doing what you were doing before anyway? It seems pointless."

"When you put it that way, it does sound pointless," Genevieve said. "But you're missing one very important part of the whole thing. The challenge of it. The ways you change, what you discover about yourself through the sacrifice of that thing or those things that you do without thinking."

Kiana shook her head. "Whatever." She looked up as they arrived at the port, walking across a short footbridge to the Canal Street Ferry. "So this is the ride, huh?"

"If you don't mind," Genevieve said. She grabbed Kiana's arm and led her through the gate and into the terminal to board the boat. "We have to hurry. It leaves soon!"

Kiana looked around as they rushed through the station. It was nondescript with white walls, gray floors, and large windows. A timeline of New Orleans provided a burst of color along the back wall of the main lobby. The timeline—a collection of paintings detailing the birth of Mardi Gras—echoed the story Genevieve told. Maskers in bright purple and yellow costumes throwing candy and trinkets, krewes on horseback waving banners and flags, jesters dancing in the street, confetti of every color swirling around it all. A day of joy and abundance before the solemn weeks of sacrifice to follow.

"You do this a lot?" Kiana asked as she boarded the ferry behind Genevieve. "Just ride the ferry for no reason?"

"Not really," she said. She led Kiana around the corner of the wide vessel and across toward the railing. The ferry was mostly empty. Only two cars had boarded on the opposite side. Three bikers, parking their bicycles against the wall of the two-story control area at the bow of the vessel, walked across the empty expanse of the ferry, settling on the very back of the ferry to lean against the railing and talk among themselves.

"So this is for me? Another touristy thing for me to experience while I'm here?" Kiana said. She grabbed the railing at the stern of the ferry as it moved away from the port. The movement was slight, the ferry gliding across the water, turning almost imperceptibly.

"Something like that," Genevieve said. She gathered the length of dress around her knees and sat carefully on the metal deck of the ferry. She let her dress drape her legs and pulled her knees against her chest and looked up at Kiana. The orange highlighted the golden flecks in her eyes, the warm glow of her smoldering honey skin.

Kiana sat beside her, crossing her legs at the ankles and playing with the loose, untied laces of her sneakers. She looked over her shoulder at the bikers then at Genevieve, who stared out at the river, a breeze rustling her short curls.

"This is nice," Kiana said. Her morning drink was wearing off, but she didn't care. She felt good.

"Yeah, you right," Genevieve said. She smiled at Kiana though something about it seemed sad.

Kiana sighed, thinking that maybe she shouldn't have divulged her mission. The ferry floated beneath twin bridges, their metallic white grates glowing against the clear blue sky. Kiana marveled at them, their symmetry, their length. The bridges seemed neat and orderly. Purposeful.

"I'm going to talk to her today," she said, looking up at the bridges as they passed underneath.

"What are you going to say?" Genevieve said.

"I don't know," Kiana said. "I've never really been good at talking about my feelings."

"I think you're better at it than you think," Genevieve said. "Open yourself up, baby, like you started to do with me." She reached out to the railing and pulled herself to her feet. She turned and looked down at Kiana. "And maybe no drinks this time. Maybe go into this conversation with a clear head, a clear heart."

Kiana sighed. She pushed herself up from the metal deck. She moved next to Genevieve and leaned against the railing. "Maybe you're right."

The ferry reached the final stop on the outbound route to Gretna. Kiana and Genevieve watched the bikers exit and the two cars. A small group of pedestrians boarded the ferry, and it began its slow turn to head back to Canal Street and the main station. Genevieve marveled at the bridges on the return trip, but something else caught her attention off the side of the ferry.

A long warehouse, filled with gigantic green and purple jester heads, orange and red plumes of feathers sticking out of glittery platforms, and oversized mirrored balls, ran the length of the riverbank.

"What's that?" Kiana asked, pointing.

"Storage," Genevieve said. "The Mardi Gras off-season." She smiled.

"It's kind of sad," Kiana said. She recalled the timeline at the station. The party captured in the paintings—the colors, the celebration, the movement. All of it crammed into a dark warehouse until next time.

"Why do you say that?"

"This amazing party just tucked away up the river. Out of sight, out of mind." Kiana shook her head. "Just stuffed into this storage space until everyone's ready to have a good time again."

Genevieve smiled and leaned into Kiana.

"What?" Kiana said.

"Oh, baby," Genevieve said. "The floats aren't forgotten or neglected." She nudged her chin toward the warehouse as the ferry moved past it, approaching the Riverwalk and terminal.

"That's valuable, important stuff. Stored away for when we need it. Every time we need it, any time we need it, there it is, in its own special place, beautiful, safe, and sound. It's like a holding place for good memories, waiting to be recalled again and again."

Kiana wanted to put her arm around Genevieve. It felt like the right thing to do after saying something so comforting, so true. But it also felt wrong. She wasn't there to get wrapped up in the warmth of this new woman, this woman who unsettled her and challenged her outlook of the world. She knew what she wanted, what she needed. She wanted and needed to talk to Michelle. To make right all the things that went wrong. Instead of seeing Genevieve as a threat to that, she should have seen her as a way to change her approach. But in changing her approach, was she changing herself?

At odds with her feelings, she playfully bumped Genevieve's shoulder and turned away from the railing.

"I'm feeling inspired. I think I'm ready," she said. She walked toward the exit. She turned to Genevieve. "Thank you," she said.

"Glad I could help," Genevieve said with a sigh.

Kiana detected a trace of disappointment in Genevieve's sigh, but dismissed it. She held out her hand for her as a gesture of friendship. Genevieve took it with a smile. Kiana squeezed her hand in response and held it as they cleared the ferry gates.

## CHAPTER SEVEN

Kiana sat at Café Du Monde sipping a hot coffee. Genevieve had been right; the coffee, strong and aromatic, was just what she needed to settle herself for her talk with Michelle. The chicory and crème in her café au lait worked just as the breeze on the ferry had; she felt peaceful and relaxed. Unfortunately, every ounce of calm drained from her the second Michelle, dressed in a button-down, salmon sundress and strappy brown sandals, came walking up to the table. Looking flirty and cool, she smiled at Kiana and pulled at the empty chair across from her. A small group of pigeons rustled around the table, cooing as they fluttered out of the way.

"Good afternoon," Michelle said. She pushed her oversized, Jackie-O sunglasses off her face and onto her head. With her hair pulled back into a loose ponytail, she looked young and fresh-faced. Her almond eyes always sparkling with mischief and a ready curve set on her glossy lips, she sighed and looked around. "Surprised you wanted to meet here."

"Why?" Kiana asked. She looked over her shoulder at the other tables. The place was busy; only a couple of empty tables were available, and everyone there sipped their coffee, munched their pastries, and brushed powdered sugar off their mouths between laughs and joyful conversation. Napkins blew around among the pigeons, and a street performing duo—two women, one on a drum machine and the other on an electric violin—provided a groove in the background.

"They don't serve alcohol," Michelle said with a shrug.

Kiana flexed her jaw. "Don't start, okay?" She had thought briefly, with the first sip of her coffee, how good it would taste with a shot or two of Maker's, the whiskey giving it just the right bite. She hadn't brought her flask, and she had promised Genevieve before she left her at the café that she would have a sober conversation. An honest, sober conversation about her feelings.

"I'm just saying," Michelle said. "It's not like you."

"Anyway," Kiana said. "Can I get you something?"

"No," Michelle said. "I'm all right. I've already had too many beignets. I've got a dress to fit into in a couple days." She giggled and pulled a bottle of water out of her large brown leather bag. She set the bottle on the table and looked around. "It's so nice out. Don't you just love New Orleans?"

"Look, let's not fuck around here," Kiana said. "What the hell is going on with you? How do you just leave me, tell me you're not coming back with a fucking text message, then five months later send me a fucking wedding invitation? A wedding invitation, Michelle. Everything about this situation is fucked up." She exhaled. She'd already messed up. She was supposed to be calm and non-confrontational.

Michelle's eyes widened. She leaned back in the green vinyl chair, the metal legs squeaking slightly. She placed a hand on her chest, just above her breasts, which were plumped in a teasing swell of cleavage at the unbuttoned collar of her sleeveless dress.

"Really, Kiana?" Michelle said. "You're going to make this about me leaving?" She spoke in a hard whisper, her eyes darting over her shoulder at the crowded tables.

"What else would it be about? You left me. Just left me and didn't come back or explain anything or—"

"So you're the victim," Michelle said. She shook her head in disbelief. "Of course you are. What was I thinking? Nothing could ever be your fault."

"What the fuck are you talking about?" Kiana placed two hands on her small coffee cup, wrapped her fingers around it to keep them from trembling. She bit at the inside of her cheek and tapped her foot. She felt a nameless but familiar frustration building. She took a deep breath. "Maybe you need to tell me what you think happened because what happened to me was that my girlfriend, my lover, my partner, left me for a vacation to visit friends then called me days later to tell me she wasn't coming back."

Michelle shook her head with a smirk. "You are pathetic, you know that? You always find a way to tell a story as if everything happens *to* you. It's like you have no responsibility for what you do, what you say. You only hear what you want to hear. I'm done letting your drunk ass rewrite history."

"What?" Kiana said. She pulled her hands back from the coffee mug, afraid she'd crush it in rage. Her face hot and jaws so tight her teeth ached, she wanted to scream.

"Do you have any idea what it was like being with you?" Michelle leaned forward. "You're broken, Kiana. The sulking, the rage, the negativity. Everything was glass half empty with you. And you kept drinking it down. I wasn't going to let you bring me down."

Kiana caught her bottom lip in her teeth and bit down hard. She cut her eyes at Michelle, wanting to grab her and shake her for the things she said, the lies. She needed to get up. She needed to break something. She needed a drink. She looked around the café. A few customers were staring in her direction, raising their eyebrows and frowning. She returned her gaze to Michelle.

"Fuck you," she said in a low grumble through clenched teeth.

"See?" Michelle said.

"See what, Michelle?" Kiana clasped her hands together beneath the table. "If I was so difficult to be with, if everything was so terrible with me, why did you stay in the first fucking place? Why even be with me at all?"

Michelle's eyes watered. "I saw something. I thought I saw something. Your passion, your creativity, your smile. I thought you'd be great. I thought we'd be great, Key."

*Key.* She hadn't heard the nickname aloud in forever. It softened her, melted the block of ice that sat in her chest. Kiana thought about when she and Michelle first met. She wanted to know her the second she saw her, struggling up the stairs with an oversized, army-issue duffle bag, a crate of books, and a pair of roller skates slung over her shoulder. Kiana put her small bag of groceries on the landing—a plastic shopping bag with two limes and a six-pack of Coronas from Dominick's—and rushed to help her.

"Moving out or in?" Kiana had asked.

"In," Michelle said. "The elevator worked when I came to look at the place. Please tell me it's just bad timing and not a regular occurrence."

Kiana laughed. "It's a very temperamental contraption. A pain in the ass, but you save a fortune on gym memberships."

Michelle rolled her teasing, dark brown eyes then smiled, her lips moist and full and made for kissing. Kiana offered to help, and without hesitation, Michelle had offered her bag and box of books to her, leading the way up the remainder of the stairs to the third floor. That afternoon, Kiana helped Michelle move into her new apartment, a floor below her own on the opposite side of the building.

"You are amazing," Michelle said. She put a hand on Kiana's shoulder, and Kiana felt the heat in her palm, the strength in her fingers. "Let me make dinner for you. As thanks."

Kiana had shrugged as if she could take it or leave it, but in reality, the touch sealed the deal. She was smitten and trying to play it cool. Out of breath and body aching, she tried to remember the last time she had done so much heavy lifting. She could barely find her voice. Her head hurt. She remembered her abandoned bag of beer and limes in the stairwell and sighed. Yet, if Michelle needed it, she would carry a hundred more boxes up a thousand more flights of stairs.

"Okay," Kiana had said. "Dinner sounds nice."

"Good! I'll make nachos," Michelle said. "Give me your beer and I'll put it in the fridge. They'll be nice and cold by the time you make your way back down here." She smiled and ran her hand down Kiana's arm.

They shared a single paper plate heavy with chips, salsa, seasoned ground turkey—Michelle didn't eat red meat—and gallons of cheese sauce. And after sipping their way through four bottles of Corona, two each, Kiana and Michelle made love in the middle of the living room, the makeshift picnic dinner serving as an appetizer for the real meal, Michelle, who was as soft and sweet and tight as she looked. While Michelle slept, on her back and gently snoring, Kiana drank the last two beers and looked out the window, already breaking her usual rules—her job and her apartment were supposed to be off limits for romance. Yet, instead of leaving, she slid behind Michelle on the floor and held her, inhaling the wild curls at the base of her neck, a spicy sweet like gardenias lulling her to sleep. Over the next few months, Kiana would slowly help Michelle move her things up one more floor.

"I thought we *were* great," Kiana said. She forced herself to push past the memory. It made her bones ache. "And so this... this Michael..." She sighed and looked away. She wanted to know how Michelle had met him. How he entered the picture. If she knew more about him, she could use him. She could blame him. And if she could blame him, she could blame Michelle. She could be a whore. A dick-riding whore who never loved her, and everything Michelle said about her could be convenient lies to shift blame.

"He's nice. We have fun together."

"I'm nice. We had fun together," Kiana said. Her mind flooded with memories of Michelle, dark hair an explosive crown of red-streaked coils, tight jeans hugging her hips, and braless breasts swelling against the faded screen print of her favorite tee as she danced and laughed, always, always throwing a glance and smile to Kiana at the bar.

"He's easy," Michelle said. She sat back in her chair. "No surprises. No disappointments. He's less complicated and less needy. He's not sad."

Kiana didn't know what to say. She felt sick. She felt tired. She couldn't fully process what was happening, what Michelle was saying to her *about* her.

"Did it ever occur to you that I needed you? That I needed your help?" Kiana's voice caught as she spoke. Tears burned her eyes.

Michelle took a deep breath and shook her head. She pulled her glasses down on her face and crossed her arms. "The kind of help you need, I can't give you." She stood and grabbed her bag from the table.

"Wait!" Kiana slammed her fist on the table. Michelle's bottle of water teetered, and several people turned in the direction of their voices. She pushed herself up from the table with so much force, her chair toppled over. Michelle looked around nervously.

Michelle sighed and shook her head. "I've got to go. I've got another appointment." She swiped at a dust of powdered sugar on the bottom of her bag.

Kiana took a deep breath, tears blurring her vision and her heart pounding in her chest. She bit the inside of her cheek. "I'm not done, Michelle. We're not done."

"Oh, Key," Michelle said. She pressed her lips together. "But we are done. We've been done for a long time. I just hope that we can be friends. I guess that's why I invited you here, to my wedding, so that we could work on that."

"I don't want to be friends," Kiana said. "I want—"

"I've really got to go," Michelle said. She turned quickly and walked away from the table.

"No!" Kiana yelled, ignoring the stares and whispers, the gawking and pointing.

But Michelle didn't stop. She slid between the tables without turning around, a wave of pigeons taking flight as she pushed through them.

## CHAPTER EIGHT

Kiana didn't remember calling Genevieve, so it surprised her when she opened her eyes to both Genevieve and the hotel bartender standing side-by-side in the last stall of the women's bathroom down the hall from the lobby.

"Genevieve," she slurred. "You're here. You came." She reached out a hand, but her arm, heavy with drunkenness, flopped back to her lap. She sat on the toilet, her pants intact, but her belt undone.

"Are you sure you have her?" the bartender said to Genevieve though he stared at Kiana, who cut her eyes at the both of them. Genevieve crossed her arms over her chest, the relaxed drape and invigorating brightness of her orange dress clashing with the tension of the moment.

"I've got myself, buddy," Kiana said. She struggled to stand, pressing one hand against the stall and gripping the toilet paper dispenser with the other.

"I've got her," Genevieve said. She put a hand on the bartender's shoulder. "Thank you for letting me come back here to get her."

"You came right on time, baby," the bartender said, shaking his head. Tall and skinny with a thin goatee, he pulled his gold vest down and stuffed his hands into his tuxedo pants. The fluorescent overhead light in the bathroom bounced off his bald head. "My manager told me to call the police." He looked down at Kiana as she continued to struggle to her feet. "Is she going to be all right?"

"I'm gonna be fucking fine," Kiana said. "And I'd appreciate it very much if you would stop talking about me like I'm not right the fuck here."

The bartender sighed and raised his hands in surrender. "Baby, good luck with this one."

"Thank you," Genevieve said.

The bartender whistled as he exhaled and shook his head at Kiana before he turned and left the bathroom.

"Can you believe that dude?" Kiana said. "Why was he even in here? This is the *women's* room. He's not even supposed to come in here. Men are not ALLOWED!" She yelled the last in the direction of the exit, her voice echoing in the empty bathroom.

Genevieve took Kiana by her arm and helped her stand. "Would you hush?" she said. She pulled at Kiana, who finally stood and leaned on her, trying to find balance on wobbly legs.

"My leg is asleep," Kiana said loudly. She stomped her foot. The pins and needles sensation made her wince. "Shit that feels weird." She laughed. "Don't you hate when that happens? When your foot or hand falls asleep? You know how it gets all tingly and shit. Crazy, right?"

Genevieve sighed. "I need you to shut up and concentrate on walking."

❖

Kiana opened her eyes and sat up in bed. The darkness of her hotel room betrayed the hour; with the heavy beige drapes pulled closed, it looked much later than five thirty in the evening. She stared at the digital clock beside the lamp and phone, trying to figure out how she got up to her room. She remembered Michelle and her teasing beauty, her unkind words, and her cruel smirk. *The kind of help you need.*

"Fuck her," she said aloud to herself. She belched and grimaced at the acidic bite of bile that jumped up her throat and burned the back of her tongue as she swallowed. She swung her legs over the side of the bed, her feet toppling the empty wastebasket set beside the nightstand. She furrowed her brows at the carefully placed puke bucket then looked around the room. The bathroom door was closed.

"Hello?" she said into the darkness. "Hello?" She pushed herself up from the bed, her head swimming and pounding at once, a ship battered by a storm, a swell of whiskey curling and crashing in the pit of her stomach.

The door opened and orange light spilled into the room. Genevieve came from around the corner of the doorjamb, a wet washcloth in her hands.

"Oh, it's you," Kiana said.

"Who else would it be?" Genevieve said. "You haven't got a single friend in this town, baby." She shook her head and walked toward Kiana. "Sit down," she said, pushing Kiana down by the shoulder.

Kiana plopped on the bed, her knees weak and back sore. "When did you get here?"

"You called me," Genevieve said. She helped Kiana lie down and placed the warm towel on her forehead. She reset the toppled bucket beside the bed.

"You know, I don't really need that," Kiana said. "I haven't thrown up from drinking since...since...shit, maybe my first time getting loaded." She closed her eyes against the warm, moist towel. At twelve, she had stolen a bottle of watermelon Boone's Farm from the corner store. She drank it all, gulping it like juice while crouching beside a trash can in the alley behind the house she lived in with Karyn and Mrs. Joyce, the old woman who took them in when their mother died. Karyn's friend Tasha, seventeen and all legs, caught her and snatched the bottle away. She threw it in the trash. Kiana cried, and Tasha pulled her into a tight hug, rubbing her back and whispering into her ear that everything would be all right. Kiana squeezed the older girl back, burying her face in the warmth of Tasha's neck. Jean Nate. Baby powder. Comfort. She had inhaled deeply and pressed her lips against the hollow of Tasha's neck. Tasha pulled back, startled. Kiana thrust her face forward and kissed Tasha on the mouth, a frantic smash of lips and teeth. Tasha pushed Kiana off her and smacked her across the face. Kiana's stomach lurched, and she had thrown up, ground chunks of Chick-O-Stick swimming in orange and red swirls at her feet.

Kiana's jaws clenched. She pressed the towel against her forehead.

"Well, you never know," Genevieve said. "Better safe than sorry, baby."

Silence filled the room, but Kiana heard her own heartbeat in her ears, the sound of her own blood rushing through her like a whoosh against her temples.

"You don't remember calling me, do you?" Genevieve said. She sat at the foot of the bed, her back to Kiana.

"No," Kiana said in a whisper. She stared at Genevieve's back, hints of firm muscle under her smooth skin, a pockmark just above one of her shoulder blades.

"I didn't think so," Genevieve said. She shifted, glancing at Kiana over her shoulder.

"You're right though," Kiana said. She took the towel off her forehead and tossed it on the nightstand. "I don't have a friend in this world." She sat up and looked across the room to the desk. A half-empty bottle of Jack Daniel's and a full bottle of Southern Comfort stood between the lamp and coffee maker. Two fresh glasses flanked the empty ice bucket, a flap of folded plastic peeking out from the lid. She sighed.

"I take it your talk with Michelle didn't go well," Genevieve said. She gripped the edge of the bed.

Kiana watched Genevieve's forearms flex. Her eyes rested on the beaded bracelets adorning her thin wrists.

"It was a terrible waste of time," Kiana said. She scooted forward on the bed. Genevieve squeezed at the bedspread. Kiana moved closer. "She's not who I remember. What I remember. Coming here for her was a mistake." She glanced at the bottles on the desk then returned her gaze to Genevieve. She inched within a breath of Genevieve. She could smell her hair, clean and fresh. Cucumber mint. She leaned in, her nose nuzzling her gentle, sandy brown curls. Her lips grazed against the nape of Genevieve's neck. "But coming here wasn't a mistake."

Genevieve shot up from the bed. She looked over at the desk. She looked at Kiana. "I've got to go," she said.

"What? Why?" Kiana turned and moved to climb out of the bed.

"No, don't," Genevieve said. Her cheeks were flushed and her breath deep and loud. She ran a hand through her short curls and bit her lip.

"I thought you liked me," Kiana said. She slouched her shoulders, shrugging and scooting back on the bed.

"I do."

"Well?"

"I've got to go," Genevieve said with a forceful sigh. She headed to the door, but Kiana, fighting the pounding in her temples and the roiling in her stomach, jumped up and grabbed her arm before she could reach it.

"Please," Kiana said. "We've already established that you're my only friend. After the day I've had, I don't want to be alone."

Genevieve shook her head and gently pulled her arm out of Kiana's grasp. She turned and walked back toward the bed. She sat. "I don't know what to do with you," she said.

Kiana grinned. "I've got some ideas."

Genevieve stood and threw up her hands. "See…"

"No, no, no," Kiana said. "I'm just playing. We can order some food. I'm hungry. Are you hungry?" She walked over to the desk, her eyes stopping on the whiskey. She opened the drawer and pulled out a small stack of menus and the hotel binder. She handed it all to Genevieve.

"I don't really have much of an appetite," Genevieve said, flipping through the folded menus. "What do you want?"

Kiana picked up the bottle of Southern Comfort then set it back down. Her fingers tapped the top of the Jack Daniel's. She took a deep breath and shrugged. She grabbed the bottle, unscrewed the cap, and poured herself two fingers of the amber whiskey. The smell seemed to dominate the room. Without turning around, Kiana knew Genevieve was watching her. She gripped the glass and brought it to her lips. She turned.

"Why?" Genevieve said. She set the menus on the bed and stood with a sigh.

"Why what?" Kiana said. She licked her lips; her tongue grazed the rim of the glass. The sharp smell of her drink prickling her nostrils.

"Why have a drink? Why have a drink now?" Genevieve's face looked pained.

"My head hurts," Kiana said. "This will help." She raised the glass with a small smirk.

"Will it?"

Kiana nodded. She brought the drink to her lips and sipped. She took a deep breath with her first swallow. The whiskey went down with a slight burn, a sweet heat sliding down into the pit of her belly. She winced. She preferred Maker's, but Daniel's was cheaper, harsher. It felt like a punishment. Maybe she wanted it to hurt.

Genevieve twisted her lips. "There will always be headaches, baby. That whiskey ain't never gonna fix it."

"You know how you said I didn't have a single friend?" Kiana said. She looked into the liquor, swirled it against the glass. "Sometimes, this is a friend. It's there. Always there. It's soothing and willing. And above all," she said, stopping to drink, draining the last of the shot, "It's nonjudgmental. It never, ever judges."

"Oh, baby," Genevieve said. She walked over to Kiana and took the glass from her hand. She set it on the desk. "I know it might seem like that, but that's not true. It's just not true. It never judges because it doesn't care. It doesn't care what you say, what you do, what you feel...even when it's hurting you." She placed her hands on Kiana's shoulders and gently moved her hands up to the sides of her face.

Tears welled in Kiana's eyes. She thought about Karyn—her gentleness, her sternness, her concern—then stopped. She swallowed and tried not to blink. She flexed her jaw against Genevieve's hands.

"Especially when it's hurting you," Genevieve said.

Kiana blinked. Two tears, one from each eye, rolled down her cheeks. She ripped herself from Genevieve's touch, and longing and loneliness gripped her instantly. She wiped at her eyes rough and fast. "Maybe you should leave."

Genevieve sighed. "I probably should." She didn't move. She looked at the Southern Comfort then across the room to the windows. "But I don't want to. I want—" She stopped.

Kiana reached out and grabbed Genevieve around her waist and kissed her. Genevieve pulled back. Kiana searched her eyes but said nothing. She leaned in, slowly, carefully. Genevieve hesitated then moved in to meet her. Kiana pressed her lips against Genevieve's and moved her hand to the back of her head, her fingers sliding through her short curls. Genevieve kissed back, opening her mouth, her entire body hot and loose in Kiana's arms. Kiana's tongue found Genevieve's, and a fierce urgency set in. Genevieve's arms wrapped about Kiana's back, and Kiana slid her hands down to the full cups of Genevieve's ass. She gripped and walked her backward toward the bed.

Fully clothed, Kiana and Genevieve rolled around on the bed, slipping thighs between thighs, rolling their hips in a slow grind. Kiana couldn't get enough of Genevieve's mouth, her dancing tongue and moist lips. Finally able to pull her mouth away, Kiana pressed hard, hot kisses underneath Genevieve's ear and down her throat. She gripped Genevieve's hips and pulled her against her thigh. Genevieve dug her hands into Kiana's afro, tugging gently and moaning, the tremble of sound in her throat making Kiana pant, unable to catch her breath. She reached her hands down and bunched up the sides of Genevieve's dress, sliding it up her thighs. Moving faster than reason, she slipped a hand between Genevieve's legs. A thin triangle of cotton met Kiana's fingertips; she shoved it aside. Hot. Wet. Throbbing.

In a rustle of movement that caught Kiana off guard, Genevieve shoved her arms out, pushing Kiana to the edge of the bed. She clamped her legs tight and scooted up toward the headboard, pulling her knees underneath her chin. She squeezed her eyes closed and ran both hands through her short hair.

"I'm sorry," Genevieve said.

Kiana jumped off the bed. "You're fucking with me, right?" She panted, her entire body hot with frustration and desire.

Genevieve shook her head. "No," she said.

"Yes, you are," Kiana said. "You're fucking with me."

"No, Kiana," Genevieve said. "I'm not fucking with you. I just need to think about this."

Kiana looked at her feet. She still had her sneakers on. She took a deep breath and clenched her fists at her side.

"Think about what, Genevieve?" she asked. She licked her lips. "That's your damn problem. Always *thinking*. Stop it. Stop thinking. Just let go for once."

"I can't," Genevieve said.

"You can. You just don't want to. You're scared." Kiana sighed. She walked around the foot of the bed to the desk. She poured another shot of Jack. "You talking all this shit, trying to get inside my head." She picked up the glass and held it by the rim, the tips of her fingers gripping the drink as she held it at her side. "Get out of my head. Get out of *your* head."

Genevieve lifted her chin and looked at Kiana. She stretched her long legs in front of her. Kiana watched her, desire still pulsing against the crotch of her panties, still full between her thighs.

"I can't afford to, Kiana," Genevieve said.

"Afford? It's not a question of affording anything." She raised her arms and stretched them out, presenting herself. She smirked. "This is free. Free and clear. I don't want anything from you." She wasn't sure what she meant with that last part. While she didn't want anything from Genevieve for real, nothing serious or intense, she did want to be close to her. She wanted to feel her, minus the clothes, touch inside her, taste her. The moment was perfect, no need to analyze it. She looked at Genevieve, her body still trembling with want, and wondered why everyone always made everything so complicated? She brought the drink to her lips and drank. She smelled Genevieve on her fingers, a teasing taste of her on the lip of the glass. Kiana's pussy clenched. She drained the whiskey, the tingling heat and bitter bite prickling her skin.

"Everything has a cost," Genevieve said, her voice a husky whisper.

Kiana laughed. "I got money. How much?"

Genevieve's eyes went stone cold. She pushed herself up from the bed and grabbed her sandals from the floor in a quick swoop. "YOU are fucked up."

"It was a joke!" Kiana said, putting the empty glass on the desk and following Genevieve to the door. "I didn't mean it like that. I was trying to lighten the mood. It was just a joke!"

Genevieve didn't say anything. She shot an icy glare over her shoulder as she yanked the door open. She shook her head and rushed toward the elevators, carrying her shoes.

"I was kidding!" Kiana came out the door and yelled the down the hall at Genevieve's back. When she didn't turn around, Kiana screamed down the hall again. "I'm sorry! Come back!"

Genevieve pushed the button to the elevator and stared at Kiana as she stepped inside to leave.

Kiana watched Genevieve go. Her eyes burning, throat dry. She returned to her room and poured herself another drink. Whiskey, no ice. She threw it back. She smelled Genevieve on her fingers still. She sucked them. She poured more whiskey. She drank it down and poured another. She held her drink in one hand while she unbuttoned her jeans with the other. She slid her hand inside her panties. She maneuvered her fingers, those same fingers that had been scorched by Genevieve's heat, and pressed them against herself. She rubbed. She wanted to rub it all away. The desire, the loneliness, the need. Fuck it all. Rub it all out and away. Without losing her rhythm, she brought her drink to her lips and gulped, deep gulps that expanded in her chest, the pressure building, her heart aching. Fuck it all.

She squeezed her eyes tight and cried out, her hips bucking, an explosion of red behind her eyes. The glass fell from her hand, but she didn't move to pick it up. She couldn't move to pick it up.

# CHAPTER NINE

*Wednesday*

Kiana climbed out of the cab and stood in the middle of the block. She glanced over each shoulder. A few cars lined the street, parked bumper to bumper, and a Harley Fatboy, shiny black and chrome with red flames painted on the gas tank leaned on its kickstand directly behind her. The sun had just risen and hadn't yet broken the tops of the duplexes and single families that lined the block. She walked up to Genevieve's bicycle and ran a finger across the cool dew that clung to the bright green frame. She took a deep breath and made her way past the main house and up the narrow cement path to the carriage house. She slowed at the sound of voices.

Genevieve's voice, low and raspy, a sexy growl almost. "You're still here."

Another voice, a woman's voice, stronger, clearer. "I told you I wasn't going anywhere."

Kiana crept closer, holding her breath. She stopped at the edge of the house and leaned against it. The moistness of the humid morning clung to the sides of the house and dampened the back of her T-shirt. She peered around the corner and into the garden. At the small, rusted wrought iron table, Genevieve stood stretching in black stretch pants and an oversized purple T-shirt that hung off one shoulder. She steadied herself on the back of one of the chairs where a woman sat sipping from a blue-checkered mug, her back half-turned to the house where Kiana stood watching. The woman pushed herself out of her chair. Big and tall, the woman wore a denim vest, her matching jeans hanging low on her waist and bunched up at the top of her black combat boots. She shrugged and shook her head, the large gold hoops in her ears shaking, too. Her hair, wavy and cropped close to her head, glimmered a shocking metallic platinum. She took Genevieve in her thick arms and held her tight, hugging her and nearly lifting her off the ground.

Genevieve's arms clasped around the taller woman's neck. She rested her head on the woman's shoulder, closed her eyes, and smiled a smile that looked like peace, looked like love.

"I'm so glad you stayed. I needed you," she said. She smiled again, her eyes still closed in private bliss.

Kiana clenched her jaws and squeezed her hands into fists. Her eyes stung. She pressed herself against the cold, wet siding of the house. She tortured herself with one last peek around the corner. Genevieve and the woman were still locked in a tight embrace. The red-haired woman kissed Genevieve on the temple, and Genevieve kissed her back, two kisses in quick succession, one on her cheek and another on her neck. An intimate touch that made Kiana sorry she had come to apologize. She should have known better. She thought Genevieve had rejected her because of a joke gone too far. That would have been an easy fix. A quick apology. Nothing was ever that simple. She should have known it was something else. It was always something else. Someone else. She took a deep breath and walked back out to the street.

She started to call a cab then decided against it. She slid her phone in her front pocket and pulled her flask out of her back pocket. Sipping whiskey and blinking back tears, she walked the long walk back to the Quarter.

# CHAPTER TEN

*Thursday*

Kiana woke up in her clothes, an empty bottle of Jack Daniel's beside her and her phone rumbling against a glass of sucked on, curled lemon wedges on the bedside table. She smacked her lips, the sour taste of whiskey and bitter lemon coating her tongue and teeth. Her head pounded. She opened her eyes and looked around the room. Light sliced into the hotel room in thin strips of golden yellow. The alarm clock read 2:07. The red dot in the corner of the display marked it afternoon. She sat up and stared at her phone. She had two missed calls from Genevieve and one from Michelle. She ran a hand over her afro, grabbing at the matted back and sides, pulling on the thick curls and knots of hair. She stood and tossed the phone on the bed. It clacked against the empty bottle.

After a hot shower, she dressed in a pair of khaki pants and black T-shirt, the last of her unworn clothes. She sat on the edge of the bed and glanced over at her phone. She picked it up and scrolled through her calls again. She stopped on Genevieve's entries for just a moment before moving on to Michelle. She pressed "call."

Michelle answered after two rings, her voice light and friendly. She apologized for having to leave so abruptly and not being prepared to talk about the past. She asked Kiana to meet her at the Montpellier Hotel, a small, two-story hotel on the outskirts of the Quarter.

"I'm not in the mood for games," Kiana said. A dull ache pulsed in her temples. She walked over to the desk and picked up the full bottle of Southern Comfort. She cracked the plastic around the cap with a twist and took a sip directly from the bottle.

"I'm not either," Michelle said. A sliding door whooshed in the background. Her voice lowered. "Just meet me, okay?"

Kiana took another sip of the sweet, syrupy liquor. The sneaking heat of it warmed her belly. She heard Michael's voice in the background. Michelle laughed away from the receiver.

"Fine," Kiana said hard and fast. "I'll meet you."

"Good," Michelle whispered then ended the call.

❖

Genevieve called three more times before Kiana switched her phone to silent and walked into the Montpellier lobby. It was small but elegant; the mahogany counters lined in gold gave the hotel an old, stately look. Dark maroon carpeting with splotches of black lead up to the check-in counter, the rest of the floor an expanse of black, burgundy, and gray marble. The gentleman behind the front desk nodded "hello" as Kiana walked past, following the carpet path to the bar.

A large glass chandelier adorned with beads, gold balls, and jagged crystals hung over a circular bar. Tall black barstools, each with a golden fleur-de-lis painted on the back, lined the curved bar. Kiana stepped up to the bar, but before she could order a drink from the petite bartender with beehive hair, Michelle called her name from a table in the corner of the lounge area.

Kiana smiled at the bartender and walked over to the dark corner table where Michelle, in a black wrap dress and chunky gold necklace, sipped from an oversized wineglass. A freshly uncorked bottle of Pinot Grigio, a little condensation dripping down the sides, sat chilled and inviting in the center of the table. Michelle lifted her hand as Kiana sat. Within seconds, a server in a white dress shirt and green bowtie brought a glass for Kiana and poured her a liberal serving of the white wine. He nodded and walked away as quickly as he appeared.

Kiana wasn't in the mood for wine. Sitting down with Michelle demanded something stronger, but she lifted the glass anyway and sipped the cool, faintly sweet wine.

"You like?" Michelle asked. She smiled. Her full lips were glossed and tinted the soft pink of litchis.

Kiana nodded. She drank from her glass once more. "It's good. Sweet, but only at first." She sipped again, holding the wine in her mouth, rolling it over her tongue before swallowing. "Then sharp and tart."

Michelle smirked. She picked up her glass. "I'm glad you agreed to come."

"Me, too. So far." Kiana drank more wine before setting her glass down slowly. She ran a hand over her afro and looked around the bar.

"You need a haircut," Michelle said. She sipped her wine. "I don't know that I've ever seen it this long. This unruly." She put her wine on the table and reached across the small table to touch Kiana's hair.

Kiana pulled back. "Yeah, well, I've been busy." She cleared her throat. She hadn't thought much about her hair—the curls and kinks locking and frizzing with a mind of their own.

"It looks good though. Wild. Free," Michelle said.

Kiana didn't respond. She stared down at her glass and turned it slowly by the stem.

Michelle sighed and poured Kiana and herself more wine. "I thought this would be easier," she said. She took a large gulp of wine. "Key, I didn't like how our talk ended at the café. I didn't want to dredge all that old shit up, you know? I wanted us to…catch up…I wanted us to just move forward."

Kiana rolled her eyes. She wished Michelle would stop calling her "Key," but liked it at the same time. She picked up her glass and drank. "I don't know why you thought we'd just pick up like everything was fine."

"I know," Michelle said. "I was being naïve. I owe you an explanation."

"Yes," Kiana said. She nodded and sipped her wine. "You do. What happened? Why did you just leave me like that?"

Michelle looked down at the table. She ran her fingers up and down the stem of her wine glass. Kiana watched her hands. She'd always loved her hands. Long, elegant fingers. Perfectly shaped, neatly trimmed nails. Her nails were longer than Kiana remembered and painted a pale, innocent pink.

"That last night," Michelle began, "we came stumbling home from the bar. Do you remember?" She met Kiana's eyes.

"Yes," Kiana lied. She didn't remember coming home from the bar. She didn't remember much about the night except that Michelle told her about visiting friends in New Orleans. "They're old friends. They just moved to New Orleans and want something familiar. I do, too," Michelle had said, nursing a Malibu and pineapple juice at their neighborhood bar.

"When we got upstairs, we argued," Michelle said. "It was stupid. You wanted to play music and dance. I was tired and wanted to sleep. I tried to take the stereo remote from you and we...we fought over it."

Kiana bit at the inside of her jaw. She tried to remember. Only flashes revealed themselves. The thump of 808's. Kelis over bass and snare beats. Light pouring in from the kitchen, making a stage of the front room. A floor lamp toppling to the carpet. The orange backlight on the stereo. The cigarette burn in the carpet like a beauty mark. More like a mole. A palm to the face. Michelle's palm. Pushing and slapping, both at once.

"I hadn't ever seen that side of you, Key. Never saw you so angry. So..."

"Hurt," Kiana said. "I was hurt." She remembered the weeks leading up to Michelle's decision to leave. Michelle had been distant, less affectionate, shrugging her way through intimate moments. When Kiana kissed her, Michelle no longer closed her eyes. Kiana never considered that there was only one way to know that.

"Things between us weren't right," Kiana said. "I didn't know how to handle it."

Michelle chuckled. "Neither one of us did," she said. She ran a finger around the rim of her wine glass. "I was going to come back," she said. "Once I got down here, I met up with my friends. We had fun. It was nice. I missed you at first."

"At first," Kiana repeated. She drank her wine, nearly draining the glass.

"I wanted to tell you I missed you those few times we talked," Michelle said. "But I wanted you to say it first. I wanted you to tell me to come home. That things could be different."

Kiana laughed. "You're a mess, you know that?" She looked around the bar, unable to meet Michelle's eyes. She threw back the last of her wine. "You watch too many movies,

Michelle." She reached for the bottle and filled her glass. She poured the last of the wine into Michelle's half-full glass.

"Well, I was confused. I wanted…" Michelle picked up her glass. "I wanted things to be different, but I didn't know what that meant. Thinking about it made me crazy. Being away from you was scary at first. As fucked up as you were, I knew I had your love. I never doubted that. But I didn't know what I wanted. I couldn't focus on me while focusing on us. I needed a break. Then I wanted direction. I thought that if you said to me, 'Come home. Let's do this thing this way and have these things,' that we could do something special. I thought that if you had a real plan, then we could be extraordinary. But you didn't have a plan. You didn't have anything."

Kiana gulped down her wine and looked over at the bartender. The woman met her eyes and nodded; her beehive hair didn't move.

"A plan?" Kiana shook her head. "The plan was to be together."

"That's not a plan," Michelle said.

As much as Kiana hated to admit it, Michelle was right. She didn't have a plan. She didn't spend too much time thinking about the future; she had a hard enough time just thinking about getting through the day. She sighed. The server appeared at the table.

"What can I get you? Another bottle?" The server, hair pulled back into a ponytail and eyes dark as charcoal, leaned forward at the waist and smiled.

"Yes," Michelle said before Kiana could answer. "And bring her a shot of Maker's."

"Very well," the server said.

"Make it a double," Kiana said as the slight man turned and headed toward the bar.

"Certainly," he said with a wink.

"Michelle," Kiana said. She placed her hands flat on the table and drummed her fingers. "None of this shit makes sense to me." She shrugged. "We could have talked about it. Just like we're doing now. Listening to the whole thing, it all sounds stupid and petty. Dramatic and..." She stopped and blew out a breath.

"I didn't know how to talk about it," Michelle said.

"So what does this mean?" Kiana said. She tried to control her tone, temper the hope and frustration caught in the back of her throat.

"I don't know," Michelle said. "I guess it means I'm sorry." She reached across the table slowly, looking into Kiana's eyes. She placed her hands on top of Kiana's. Kiana didn't move.

"Playing it back, it is silly. It's all very dumb." Michelle rubbed the tops of Kiana's hands, scratching her nails down her fingers then tracing her knuckles with her fingertips. "And I'm sorry. I'm sorry for not talking to you about what I felt. What I wanted."

Kiana's stomach tingled. Her mouth watered. She moistened her lips with her tongue. She wanted to move her hands, but couldn't. She swallowed and watched Michelle's fingers move over her knuckles, reaching up toward her wrists. Michelle's hands felt nice. Her touch was always a comfort. She shook her head against memory, blurring recollections of touch, care, and hurt. The server returned with another bottle of wine and Kiana's double shot. Kiana yanked her hands away as he set the drink and bottle down. She and Michelle leaned back in their chairs as he uncorked the wine and refilled Michelle's glass. He left the bottle on the table and nodded before walking away.

Michelle held up her glass and smiled. Kiana lifted her drink.

"I feel better," Michelle said. "Do you?"

Kiana didn't know how she felt. The anxiety that lined the walls of her stomach surged and blazed. The cavernous need that hollowed her heart yawned in her chest. She gripped her drink and stared into Michelle's eyes, looking for something though she wasn't sure what exactly. Longing? Regret? Love?

"Sure," Kiana said, forcing a smile.

Michelle grinned and raised her wine. "Let's just leave it all in the past, Key."

"To moving on," Kiana said. She tipped her drink in Michelle's direction.

"Cheers," Michelle said. She sipped her wine.

Kiana killed her double shot and slammed the glass on the table.

"Well, damn!" Michelle said with a laugh.

Kiana laughed, too. She raised her hand in the direction of the bartender, who smiled and nodded once again.

❖

The lounge was nearly empty, and the music switched from energetic big band to smooth jazz, the slow whining of a saxophone against the soft synthetic rhythm of a drum machine and tinkling keyboard. Michelle poured the last of her wine, draining the second bottle, into her glass. Kiana stared down at her fourth double shot of Maker's. Her eyelids heavy, her body loose, she leaned over the table, resting her chin on her fists, practically holding up her head.

"I think I always knew," Kiana said. She blinked slowly and twisted her lips. "I always fucking knew you would leave me for some man."

"Now wait a minute," Michelle said, her voice soft and slurred. "I don't appreciate that shit, Key." She shook her head and wagged her finger at Kiana.

"Bisexuals," Kiana said, "Always leave for a man at the end of it all. You're all scared. Can't hang. It's okay, buddy. I get it. Being a lesbian is hard fucking work."

Michelle blew air through her lips. "Woe is me," she said. She took a big swallow of wine. "Poor little rich girl. Beautiful women falling all over me. Live-in pussy at the drop of a dime. Fucking and fighting just to fuck again. Yeah, lesbians have it so hard." She slapped at Kiana's arms then drank more wine.

"Whatever. It ain't like that," Kiana said. She sipped her whiskey and tried to focus her eyes. "It's the people. Society. People hate us. They judge us. Want to fix us. I don't need to be fixed. I'm not fucking broken, bitch!" She said the last with venom, spit flying as she continued. "Fuck it. I don't care. Leave. Avoid the judgment of the masses. Hide in your straight safety!"

"I've been judged, too!" Michelle said. She slapped her hand on the table. The bartender looked in their direction then shook her head.

Kiana put a finger over her mouth. "Quiet down," she whispered against her wet lips. "We're scaring the white people."

Michelle and Kiana burst into laughter. Michelle covered her mouth, her shoulders shaking as she giggled into her palm. Kiana chuckled into her fist.

Michelle caught her breath then grabbed her glass to drink the last of her wine. She looked at Kiana. "You know me, Key," she said. Her voice low and serious, she continued, "You know I never gave a fuck about what people thought of me."

She scooted her chair around the side of the table. Clumsy, but quick, she stopped Kiana from taking another sip of her drink. She took the glass out of Kiana's hands and placed it on the table.

Kiana stared at her. She blinked and furrowed her eyebrows. She whispered, "What do you want from me?"

Michelle leaned in, her lips hovering close to Kiana's. Her breath was hot. Woodsy and fruity at the same time, both heavy and light at once. Kiana could taste it. Could taste her. She closed her eyes, remembering. Michelle moved forward, pressing her lips against Kiana's mouth. The heat of the kiss was familiar, the high of it brand new. Michelle's tongue pushed through the forbidden darkness, sparked the blazing duplicity of it. The ache of time passed and love remembered burst between them. Kiana accepted it all, ready and willing to be burned by the fire of it all. She sucked at Michelle's tongue, and Michelle pulled back with a gasp. She put her hands to her mouth and pushed herself back, her chair screeching against the marble floor.

"I'm sorry," Michelle said. She stood, still holding her fingers to her mouth.

"You don't have to be," Kiana said. She swallowed hard and looked up at Michelle, who trembled before her, eyes wide with surprise and fear. Kiana reached out to her, but she took a step back.

"That was a mistake," Michelle whispered. Her voice was muffled behind her fingertips. "I didn't mean to do that. That wasn't right." She shook her head.

"But it was," Kiana said. "It was right. We're right. It was right before, and it can be right again."

Michelle kept shaking her head. She took her purse from the back of her chair and clutched it to her chest. "I'm going to go pay and…" She took a deep breath and backed away from Kiana. "I'm going to pay and get back. It's late. And I'm sure Michael is waiting up for me. I should go." She turned and walked toward the bar. She stopped.

Kiana stood up.

Michelle turned. "We're cool, right?"

Kiana's shoulders slumped. She didn't speak. She picked up her glass and drank the last swallow of whiskey. She clutched the glass and set it down, keeping her fingers wrapped around it.

"Key," Michelle said. "We're good, right? Say we're good."

Kiana bit the inside of her cheek. "Yeah," she said. "We're good."

Michelle smiled. Kiana watched her chat with the bartender while she paid the tab. Michelle glanced at Kiana over her shoulder before taking her cell phone out of her handbag. Kiana felt sick, whiskey and wine bubbling up and burning the back of throat. She swallowed it down and waved at Michelle when she nodded her good-bye and walked out of the lounge, her phone pressed against her face, the curve of her lips as she spoke to what could only be *her Michael* already making a dream, a nightmare, a memory, of the kiss they shared.

# Chapter Eleven

*Friday*

Kiana left three messages for Karyn. Two on her cell phone and one on her work phone. She needed to talk to someone. She couldn't trust anyone. Not even herself. Her lips still burned from kissing Michelle, and though Genevieve left messages and sent texts trying to reach her, she didn't want to talk to her either. Seeing her with that other woman deepened her confusion. For all the emotional shit Kiana tried to avoid, she found herself an absolute wreck, a sordid mess of hopes and desires, disappointment and confusion.

She sat at the hotel bar, spinning her phone and staring at the television, a suspended flat screen in the upper corner of the bar. *SportsCenter*, talking heads and streaming headlines, slow-motion dunks and replayed fouls, was something for Kiana to look at to avoid looking at herself. Her phone rang. She looked at the name. She didn't want to answer it, but Genevieve's calls were the only ones ringing her phone.

"Hello," she said.

"Finally," Genevieve said. "Why haven't you been answering my calls? I've been worried about you, baby! I didn't know if you had gone back to Chicago or if you—"

"What do you want, Genevieve?" Kiana said, cutting her off. She ordered another beer with a nod toward to the bartender. He pursed his lips and shook his head, flipping a towel over his shoulder and going into the cooler to grab another Heineken. The bartender, a scarecrow thin man with a shiny bald head and thin moustache and tiny, neatly-lined beard had greeted her like he knew her, asking her if she was feeling better, but Kiana shrugged it off with a dismissive smile.

"I want to talk," Genevieve said. "Like I said, I was worried."

"You ain't got to worry about me," Kiana said.

"What's wrong?" Genevieve asked.

Kiana said nothing. She stared up at the screen. Two bald men in checkered blazers and loud, florescent double-Windsored ties, pointed and shook their heads at each other. Numbers and names flashed along the bottom of the screen.

"Is it Michelle?" Genevieve said.

"No."

"What is it then?"

"I'm not sure I want to talk about it," Kiana said.

"That's exactly why we should," Genevieve said. "There's a restaurant called Mother's. Meet me there. Let's talk. Eat and talk. You can tell me what your problem is while I inhale a po' boy." She chuckled. Kiana remained silent.

"Are you upset with me? If so, that's kind of backward ain't it, baby? You're the one who—"

"Mother's?" Kiana said, interrupting Genevieve and raising her hand toward the bartender.

"Yeah." Genevieve cleared her throat. "It's on Poydras."

"I'll be there in an hour." Kiana ended the call before Genevieve could respond. "A shot of Jack. And don't be shy."

❖

Kiana stepped out of the cab and stood on the corner, taking in the two-story brick relic that was Mother's restaurant. It was busy. People huddled in small groups around the covered entrance, some with complimentary maps from hotels in the Quarter, others laughing and lighting cigarettes while leaning against the railed ramp leading to the door, all of them negotiating next stops. The afternoon, warm and bright, held promise for them. Kiana squinted against the sun and finger-picked her afro as she negotiated her own next steps. She wasn't sure what to say to Genevieve. She recalled the woman she caught her with, and the evening before that when they got hot and heavy in her hotel room. Having kissed Michelle, everything felt set on an edge, one wrong move and she'd fall into oblivion.

Kiana entered the restaurant. Genevieve sat at a small table near the bustling register. The place buzzed with people and burst with smells. Kiana slid between bodies and pulled out a stool at the counter that ran along the windows facing the street. She sat down with a plop. She cut her eyes at Genevieve, who grinned then frowned.

"I don't know what to make of your body language, baby," Genevieve said. "I certainly didn't like how you treated me on the phone. I'm hungry, but I want to get to the bottom of your attitude. What's your problem?"

"I don't have a problem," Kiana said.

"Bullshit," Genevieve said. She leaned forward and adjusted herself on the stool, her breasts jiggling against her fitted T-shirt. The baby blue shirt, a determined UNC ram strutting across the front, made her look sporty and energetic.

Kiana shrugged. "So, what's good here?" she asked. She looked around the place. A long line snaked from the register and metallic counter where hungry patrons pointed at food steaming in stainless steel troughs. She caught sight of the chalkboard over the grills but couldn't make out anything on it. She glanced around at other people's plates and the trays steadied on the shoulders of dashing servers.

"Everything," Genevieve said. "But you don't get to eat until you tell me what the hell is going on. Why wouldn't you take my calls? Why ignore me? I'm the one who should be mad at you, baby. Your joke the other night? Not. Funny." She pursed her lips and crossed her arms.

"I'm sorry about that," Kiana said. Genevieve was cute when she was mad. Her dark, smoldering honey eyes and perfect eyebrows, challenge and irritation dancing at the corners of her full mouth. She smelled good. Clean cucumber and sharp mint, something floral, too, but it wrestled with the smell of ham, gravy, and shrimp in the restaurant. Kiana felt her thoughts wandering, the hefty shot and beers she'd had keeping her from settling on any one thing too heavily. "It really was just a joke. I was out of order though. I'm sorry."

Genevieve raised an eyebrow. "I don't even know why I care."

Kiana balked. "I don't know why either," she said, standing up. "This was a bad idea. I don't even know what I'm doing here. This long ass line. You're from here and you bring me to this tourist trap." She looked around the restaurant. A server whizzed by with a tray holding two shrimp po' boys and a bowl of gumbo, a neat serving of rice accenting the deep brown stew inside. Kiana stepped aside.

"Wait." Genevieve scooted forward on the stool and rested her hands on her knees. "What am I missing?"

"I saw you with your girlfriend," Kiana said. She stuffed her hands in her pockets.

"What?" Genevieve looked up at Kiana. "What are you talking about? Here, sit down," Genevieve said. She smacked the vinyl seat.

Kiana glanced around the restaurant and down at the empty seat beside Genevieve. She sighed, shrugged, and sat down slowly, her body feeling loose.

"You acted all offended about my joke when you were really just feeling guilty," Kiana said. "You got caught up and needed to make a mad dash before you did something you would regret in the morning."

Genevieve screwed up her face and ran a hand through her curls.

"I saw the two of you together. I came by to apologize and saw you making out with some Sasquatch ass motorcycle dyke with Sisqo hair."

Genevieve burst into laughter. She laughed so hard her face flushed with a deep pink that rose from her cheeks and engulfed her nose. She doubled over, gasping.

"What the fuck's so funny?" Kiana said. She looked around, annoyed. People stared at her and Genevieve, simple smiles and wide eyes.

Genevieve finally caught enough breath to speak. "Oh Lawd! Baby! You say you saw me and—" She chuckled some more.

"I saw you and your super stud motorcycle gang girlfriend making out in your garden! Shit, the more I think about it, you owe me an apology." Kiana folded her arms across her chest.

Genevieve stopped laughing. "What?"

"I said, you owe me an apology."

"How you figure that?"

Kiana sighed. "I don't know," she said. Her face flushed with heat.

Genevieve reached and placed her hand on Kiana's forearm. "How you figure that?"

Kiana swallowed hard. "You've been so nice to me. Almost like you've been looking out for me. If I didn't know any better, I'd think you were…I don't know…liking me a little bit."

Genevieve took her bottom lip between her teeth and looked away. She returned her hand to her lap. She turned to Kiana. "Honestly? I was, but you're here for something else. For someone else."

"But let's say I wasn't. What if I was here for you? To meet you?" Kiana spun on the stool, facing the window, dozens of framed pictures crowding around the panes. She flicked at the blinds. Sunlight fought its way into the restaurant. Stripes of light warming the Formica and glinting off the stainless steel detail of the counters, tables, and chairs. "You said you don't believe in coincidences."

Genevieve bowed her head and took a deep breath. Kiana didn't know what to make of the gesture. She waited for her to speak, to lift her eyes.

"Taz isn't my girlfriend," Genevieve said.

"Taz?" Kiana chuckled.

"Yeah," Genevieve said. "She isn't my girlfriend. I don't know what you saw, but we weren't making out. Trust me, baby."

"Whatever. It don't really matter anyway." Kiana looked over her shoulder at food line, trying once again to make out the options on the chalkboard menu.

"Taz is my sponsor," Genevieve said. "And you're right. It doesn't matter."

"Sponsor?" Kiana looked at Genevieve. Her whiskey from earlier rumbled in her stomach. Suddenly self-conscious, she placed a hand on her abdomen to settle her stomach. Not drinking was one thing; being in Alcoholics Anonymous was another. She pulled at the collar of her black T-shirt.

"Sponsor." Genevieve's eyes meeting Kiana's dead-on.

"I'm..." Kiana paused, unsure of what to say, unsure she should even say anything. Apologies came second nature to her, but she couldn't be certain what she was sorry about in that moment. "I didn't know."

"How could you?" Genevieve said. She stood. "These last few days have been difficult for me, baby."

"I'm sorry," Kiana said.

"What are you apologizing for?" Genevieve said.

Kiana hesitated. "I don't know. The joke? Drinking around you? I don't know. I'm confused." Her stomach griped, a ball of nausea with an ache in the center. "There's always so much to apologize for."

"Yeah, you right." Genevieve sighed. She put her hands on her small hips. "Your joke wasn't my biggest problem, Kiana. It was me. I felt myself losing control. I can't let that happen." She turned to survey the line, which despite its constant movement, never seemed to shorten.

"I don't know what to say," Kiana said. She joined Genevieve as she walked toward the food line.

"You don't have to say anything."

Kiana took a place in line behind Genevieve who moved to file in behind a small family of three, two teenage girls with long brown hair and braces who were yanking on their father's arms and squealing about crawfish étouffée and red beans.

"Maybe we shouldn't spend any more time together," Kiana said. She held her breath. She didn't want Genevieve to agree though she knew it might be best.

"I thought about that," Genevieve said. "Taz thinks I should forget I ever found you that night."

"You didn't 'find' me," Kiana said taking in air then blowing it loud and slow.

"Whatever, baby," Genevieve said, rolling her eyes. "She thinks you're bad for me."

The line inched forward. The smells that weaved between the bodies in the dining room did more than waft beneath their noses now that Kiana and Genevieve were nearly face-to-face with the cooking stations. The heavy aroma of gravy, roast beef, baked ham, shrimp, and sausage grabbed them about the face, hooking their nostrils and pulling them closer and closer to grills, ovens, and steaming piles of rice, beans, and okra.

"What do you think?" Kiana said. Finally able to read the menu, her eyes latched on to the Ferdi Special. A cook held a plate with a two French bread halves topped only with lettuce and began preparing one right in front of her. He covered the bed of crispy green with steaming ham and juicy beef, gravy dripping from each pinch of meat. He put the tops on the sandwich and passed the plate to another cook who scooped red beans into a small Styrofoam cup and placed it on the plate beside the overflowing sandwich.

"I already told you," Genevieve said. She too watched the cooks prepare plates of food. "I don't believe in coincidences, baby." She shot a glance over her shoulder and gave Kiana a small smile.

Kiana went silent. Her stomach hurt, and the ache had nothing to do with hunger pangs. She touched her lips and remembered Michelle's kiss. The all-too familiar softness, the full-bodied sweetness that used to be all she ever needed. She wanted it still. She needed it still. She watched Genevieve, who spoke with one of the cooks as if they were old friends. Her beauty effortless, her spirit open and inviting. She had been jealous when she saw her with the stud woman; she had fought the urge to kick the woman's motorcycle over, fantasized about it clanging against the cement. She dismissed those feelings rather quickly. She moved on to what she knew, what was familiar, what made sense. Michelle. With the kiss, she had a chance to complete her mission. She could reclaim what was hers and make everything right again.

Kiana ordered the Ferdi Special after Genevieve placed her order for a shrimp po' boy and a side of red beans. They made their way over to the counter and sat on two stools a few seats down from where they were originally. They waited for their food in silence. Kiana fiddled with the bottles on the counter in front of her, hot sauce, ketchup, and peppers. She moved them about like a three card monte, wanting to say something but not willing to take the risk of saying the wrong thing.

"I don't understand you, Kiana." Genevieve rested her elbow on the counter. "I want to, but I can't. Maybe I'm intrigued by the challenge."

Kiana found a peeling corner on the hot sauce label. She flicked it with her index finger.

"I don't know why we *ran* into each other. And that night in the Quarter—" Genevieve stopped. "Never mind."

"Don't wrack your brain on it, Genevieve," Kiana said. "Most times, I don't understand myself." Kiana shrugged. She looked around, searched the menu and the tables. Sweet tea and lemonade, soda and water. Her eyes scanned each table, each tray. Two women, picking off each other's plates and giggling, ignored their nearly full glasses of wine. A woman and man at another table, silently chewing and staring over each other's shoulders, each picked up their beers at the same time and shared a smile at the synchronized movement.

"I'm going to order a beer," Kiana said. She slid off her stool and left Genevieve behind, and as she made a beeline for the register in hopes of placing a quick drink order, she felt Genevieve's soulful eyes on her, reaching and following, demanding and pushing. Sweat tickled her skin, and a warmth washed over her. She swallowed and clenched her fists. A small group of women huddled at the cash register smiled and chuckled as Kiana charmed her way in front of them, ordering her beer and commenting on how exciting it was to be in New Orleans for the first time. The women, all from Wisconsin, cracked jokes about beer being a lunchtime staple, maybe even worthy of its own food group. Kiana laughed with them before wishing them a pleasant rest of their visit.

She made her way back to the counter, her sandwich waiting for her, and sat on the stool. Genevieve eyed her beer as she set it down then picked around on her shrimp po' boy. She forked a tender piece of shrimp and brought it to her mouth slowly.

"What?" Kiana said. "I'm sorry, but I was dying over here. Is this okay?"

"You're fine," Genevieve said.

Kiana sipped her beer, licking frothy suds from her top lip. The buzz of her previous shots had warmed her, and she needed to cool down. The beer would do just that. She knew she was being insensitive, but she reminded herself of her dinner with Genevieve when she had brought her own wine. Alcohol was Genevieve's struggle, not hers. She had everything under control.

Genevieve ate more shrimp. Kiana picked up her fork and went to work with her sandwich. It was so heavy with gravy, she didn't dare pick it up. She tasted the beef, swiping at the gravy and debris, bits of meat mixed into the gravy, which spilled onto the plate.

"I think my eyes were bigger than my stomach," she said.

"Might be an understatement, baby," Genevieve said.

"What you mean by that?" Kiana said before plucking a piece of baked ham from her sandwich and placing it on her tongue.

"Be honest with me for once, Kiana. Be honest with yourself," Genevieve said. She ate another piece of shrimp and grabbed the hot sauce. "There is a reason you came to meet me for lunch. And it wasn't just to throw my sponsor in my face."

"I thought it was your girlfriend," Kiana said. She drank from her beer.

"She wasn't. She isn't. But what difference does it make?"

Kiana sighed. The beer was good, heady and full in her mouth, though it wasn't quite strong enough to deal with the type of conversation Genevieve attempted between bites of shrimp and red beans.

"I don't know," Kiana said with a shrug. But she did know. She was no stranger to the feelings that skittered around in her chest when she saw Genevieve with that other woman. Jealousy. Anxiety. Anger. Doubt. Uncertainty. As she ran through the list of feelings, she saw them, burned into her chest, each letter on fire. A brand. She felt them all the time. They never went away, never subsided. Maybe Genevieve wasn't even the point. She drank her beer and imagined dousing the blazing words with the cool, amber liquid. Sizzle. Smoke. When it clears, everything is fine.

"You can't have it both ways, baby," Genevieve said.

"I know," Kiana said. She started to say more but drank from her beer instead. She stared at her food. She picked at the meat with her fingers, brought a pinch of ham and beef to her lips, then stopped.

"I don't want it both ways," she said, returning the meat to her plate. "Most of the time, if I really, really think about it, I don't know what the hell I want." She took a deep breath, the act of telling the truth making her feel small, afraid even. "Take you, for example. You're beautiful. You're smart and sexy and—" She stopped. "I like you. I know I do. I hated seeing you with that woman. I wanted to make love to you in my hotel room that night."

Genevieve smiled and looked away. She nodded and exhaled loudly while reaching for her glass of water. She drank from it, silent but watching Kiana all the while. Her light eyes encouraged Kiana, the way the light that crept through the blinds reflected something like hope and trust, love and understanding.

"Then I think about Michelle, her wedding, and what I think I want or thought I wanted." Kiana stopped. She pinched at the meat of her po' boy again.

"Maybe you need to just step back from everything," Genevieve said. She picked up her paper napkin, and wiped her mouth. "Me, Michelle, all of it, baby. Just take some time for yourself. Figure your own shit out before you even start thinking about your feelings for Michelle or…your feelings for me." She smirked a little and shook her head.

"What? Why'd you smile like that?" Kiana placed the thick pinch of ham and beef into her mouth. She closed her lips around her fingers slowly, sucking the gravy with bits of debris from her fingertips. She chewed and reached for her beer.

"It's just these deep conversations about feelings and everything," Genevieve said. "You'd think our hearts been dancing around each other for years. My heart ain't danced in a good while, baby, and I'm not sure I can catch your beat."

Kiana smiled. The poetry with which Genevieve spoke struck her every time. She sipped at her beer and ate more of her sandwich. There was far more of it than she could dream of finishing, and between the hearty helping of meat, bread, and gravy, the fullness of the beer, she felt stuffed, her stomach tight.

She looked over at Genevieve, who despite her thin, athletic figure, continued to munch enthusiastically at her shrimp po' boy, staring at her plate as if deep in thought. Kiana wanted her to continue. She needed to hear more poetry. Perhaps there would be answers in Genevieve's stanzas; maybe her lyrics could unlock the secrets Kiana seemed to subconsciously hide from herself.

"Genevieve," Kiana said. She pushed her plate away then wrapped her fingers around her nearly empty glass of beer. She focused on the liquid inside. The sparse suds hugging the edges of the beer. She met Genevieve's eyes, the dark amber of them as cool, as smooth, as intoxicating as the beer she held in her hands.

"Yes?" Genevieve said.

"Thank you," Kiana said. She didn't feel drunk, but she knew she wasn't exactly sober. She turned to face the counter. She closed her eyes and tried to remember the last time she had actually been sober. She couldn't recall. She'd been drinking every day. Every single day for as long as she could remember. She opened her eyes and clutched her glass.

"You don't have to thank me," Genevieve said. She placed her hand on Kiana's thigh. "Just think about what's happening. Think about what has happened and what has yet to happen. They all work together, baby."

"What works together?" Kiana frowned, her eyes fixated on her beer.

"Past, present, and future," Genevieve said. "It's like a combination lock. The numbers, that's what we know. The past. We can know it. But it don't mean nothing if we don't do something with them, if we don't spin them numbers in the right order. But when we do, baby, everything opens up for us." She squeezed Kiana's thigh.

"A combination lock, huh?" Kiana said. "That's a good one."

"One of my nana's favorite metaphors," Genevieve said.

Kiana shook her head and picked up her beer. She looked down at Genevieve's hand, and instead of desire, something else grabbed her. The feeling of hands. A hand on a shoulder. A leg. Soothing circles in the center of her back. She thought of Karyn's hands. Long fingers. Creased knuckles. Veins crisscrossing along the top.

"You've got old hands," Kiana had told Karyn once. They sat in the darkness. The basement of the house Kiana remembered growing up in. Mrs. Joyce's house. Call-me-Mrs.-Joyce-not-grandma's house. Mrs. Joyce had died. Left the house and everything in it to Karyn. The sound of feet above their head. Mahalia Jackson's haunting voice rising above the murmuring voices.

"I've got Mama's hands," Karyn had said. She rubbed them together then held them out. Kiana took them in her own trembling hands. Flipped them over.

"They're nice hands," Kiana said. Tears attacked her eyes, the piercing burn of a thousand spears.

Karyn pulled her into her arms and held her. The memory faded. The embrace a precursor to a promise to join the other mourners upstairs, the promise to eat something, the promise to clean herself up. On her way to the bathroom, she caught a glimpse of neighborhood boys outside the back door smoking and passing a paper-bagged bottle of something between them. Their faces somber and tight against the cold. Their breath puffs of hot mist against the November chill. She hadn't made it to the bathroom, and even though the men didn't want to share their drink, told her she was too young, the streaks of dried tears and trembling in her chin compelled them. They shared. She drank. And drank. And drank.

An ambulance screamed past. Genevieve lifted her hand abruptly, and Kiana jumped. She watched as Genevieve crossed herself and muttered something under her breath.

"Another habit from your nana?" Kiana asked. She said it quietly, her voice a whisper as if she'd truly traveled into her past, the thousand miles back to Chicago, her throat tired and raw from the cold of that back porch and the burn of Wild Turkey.

"Something like that," Genevieve said. "It's a blessing. For whoever got themselves jammed up in that ambulance. Hope they can get fixed up, and if not, safe travels from this world to the next."

"Safe travels," Kiana repeated. She peered through the blinds though the ambulance had long gone, the siren as faint as all her memories.

"Yeah," Genevieve said. She returned her hand to Kiana's thigh. "It's a small thing, but it means a lot." She squeezed. "Do you know what I mean, baby?"

Kiana, holding her beer in one hand, placed the other on top of Genevieve's hand. She looked at her own hand, thinking again of Karyn, which meant thinking of her mother, thinking of comfort and safety. She denied herself the memory of care; she drank up those memories and submerged them into darkness with everything else. It didn't have to be that way. Genevieve, more than anyone ever before, showed her that it didn't have to be that way. Maybe she was starting to get it.

"It's a well-wishing either way. Live or die, be well," Kiana said.

"Exactly." Genevieve smiled at her.

"I'll drink to that," she said. She lifted her glass and gulped the last of her beer.

## CHAPTER TWELVE

Kiana folded her clothes slowly and carefully placed them in her bag. She looked at the clock on the nightstand. She had returned from lunch with Genevieve with a resolve of steel. She needed to go home. They hadn't had a formal good-bye, she and Genevieve, but they both knew it was best. Genevieve had pulled her into a hug, pressed her face in the crook of her neck, and whispered against her skin that it was best that she go. Kiana knew it. She nodded and squeezed Genevieve tight, an understanding settling in her bones. She needed to step back; she needed to talk to Karyn and sort things out. There was nothing else to be done.

Michelle was getting married in two days. Her feelings for Genevieve were too complicated at best, convenient at worst. Kiana lifted a T-shirt and smelled it. It stank of sweat and booze and smoke. She rolled it up and stuffed it in a corner of her duffle bag reserved for worn panties and socks. She looked around the room and sat on the bed. She swiped her phone from the nightstand. Karyn still hadn't called. Kiana had left three messages for her during the cab ride from Mother's to the hotel. She was ready to come home. She needed to come home.

A series of short, sharp knocks sounded at the door. Kiana jumped. She tossed her phone on the bed.

"Who is it?" she said, creeping toward the door.

"Room service," a male voice said.

"I didn't order any room service," Kiana said. She stopped at the door and peered through the peephole. A young man in black slacks, gold vest, and white collared shirt stood cradling a covered ice bucket in his arms. He knocked again and Kiana pulled back from the door.

"Room service for Kiana Lewis," the young man said.

Kiana peered through the hole again. The man sighed, smacking on gum and rolling his eyes. He looked at his watch.

"Look," he said, "I'll leave it outside the door. It's paid for." He popped his gum impatiently and leaned forward, cutting his eyes and looking into the peephole himself.

Kiana pulled the door open. "I didn't order anything," she said.

"Well, someone did." The man shrugged and stood awkwardly, tapping his fingers on the side of the bucket and rocking back on his heels. He raised his neat, arched eyebrows and flipped a swoop of chestnut brown bangs off his forehead.

Kiana stood back and let him enter her room. He set the bucket on the desk and looked around. "Checking out?"

"Tomorrow morning," Kiana said.

The skinny man shrugged and popped his gum. He slid a steak knife, a lime, and a small container of salt out of his vest pocket and set it on the desk next to the bucket. "Enjoy," he said with a tight smile.

He left the room. Kiana glanced at the desk. An opened, but nearly full, bottle of Southern Comfort sat in the corner near the lamp; two clean glasses and an empty ice bucket crowded the opposite end of the desk near the hotel services binder and notepad. The newly placed bucket, still covered by a white linen napkin, sat near the edge of the desk flanked by the knife, lime, and glass salt shaker. She walked over to the desk and picked up the knife. Her cell phone sang and buzzed. A text message. Clutching the knife, she went over to her phone.

Michelle's message was simple: *Get yourself in the mood.*

Kiana smirked and shook her head. She looked over at the bucket. Without lifting the napkin, she knew full well what was in it. She knew by the lime and salt that it was tequila, but from Michelle's message, she knew it was Cuervo.

Jose Cuervo was the one liquor Michelle drank beside Malibu, which to Kiana wasn't much of a liquor at all. Michelle had brought out a bottle of Cuervo one cold winter afternoon in February. The hawk was in full force, the wind chill well below ten degrees. The weatherman warned people about the bitterness of the day, urging people to stay inside unless absolutely necessary. Kiana and Michelle huddled beneath covers and kept each other warm against the clacking of the overworked but underperforming radiator in their apartment. Michelle had jumped up and dashed into the kitchen, her thermal pants sagging on her small behind and her sweatshirt swallowing her petite shoulders and thin arms.

"I hope you're thinking what I'm thinking," Kiana had said. Michelle shot a quick glance over her shoulder and ordered her to get more blankets.

"Make my cocoa Irish. If you know what I mean," Kiana said pushing herself off the couch and going into the bedroom for more blankets. She stomped her feet until her jogging pant legs met her ankles, and she stuffed her hands into the pouch of her hoodie. She pulled the comforter off their bed and rolled it up to carry it into the front room. Music blasted from the living room, Beres Hammond's "Rockaway" chasing away the dullness of the gray afternoon. Kiana had dropped the blanket and found Michelle in the front room, her sweatshirt and thermal pants flung across the leather chair. She rolled her body to the saxophone and electric guitar of the Jamaican riddim. Her white tank top rode up on her taut belly; her long caramel legs flexed and stretched out from royal blue panties. She clenched a wedge of lime between her teeth and carefully moved her arms as she held two shots of golden tequila in each hand.

"I didn't even know we had that," Kiana had said, pulling her hoodie off and pushing her sweatpants down her thighs. She joined Michelle in the center of the living room, the radiator hissing and ticking, the windows shuddering from the freezing wind cutting across the lake and colliding with the window of their third floor apartment. Her skin flushed at the scent of Michelle, the spicy-sweet breath of gardenias, and even in her white v-neck T-shirt and black boy-shorts, Kiana felt enveloped in warmth. She took one of the shots and leaned in to kiss Michelle, who passed the wedge of lime from her mouth to Kiana's with a pinch that sent sharp, tart juice dripping between both their lips. When Kiana secured the wedge in her own mouth, Michelle smiled.

"I'm full of surprises," Michelle had said, downing her shot in one gulp.

Kiana had followed suit. They did two more shots before fucking to the point of exhaustion, sweaty, hot, heavy exhaustion in the middle of the floor.

Kiana's phone rang and vibrated again, bringing her out of the memory. Michelle again. An address, then: *My last night of freedom.*

## CHAPTER THIRTEEN

Kiana leaned on her elbows at the bar and watched the door while bobbing her head to the hypnotic beats blasting overhead. She hadn't ordered anything. She didn't need to. The gritty burn of tequila and lime still tickled the back of her throat and slowed her pulse, the muscles of her heart moving in waves instead of beats. She didn't register the people around her, the few people lining the bar, the small groups in collections of lifted hands, stomping feet, and rolling torsos. A couple fell into the bar from the street. They stood in the doorway, linked arm in arm, their heads on a swivel. Laughing and slapping each other's arms, they finally cleared the doorway. Kiana pushed herself off the bar.

Genevieve stood at the entryway of the club. Everything around her dissolved into a blurry mix of colors, an abstract painting where only her form, defined and disarming, was captured with clear, indisputable lines. Her sleeveless dress fondled every curve of her hips and thighs, the white sheath stopping a few inches above her knees. She ran a quick, nervous hand across the bows of clavicle beckoning from the scooping boat neck of her dress. Having traded her casual ensembles of khaki skirts, halter tops, and sandals, she looked taller and more elegant than Kiana could have imagined. She walked toward Kiana, who finally made her feet work and met her halfway.

"You look absolutely...amazing," Kiana said. She wished she could think of another word, something more descriptive, more impressive, more accurate. Drinking Genevieve in from head to toe once again, finally taking in the grace in her shapely lips and the brilliance of her smoldering honey eyes, she became certain the word hadn't been invented yet.

"Thank you," Genevieve said. She brought her hands together in front of her and clasped her silver pocketbook with both hands. "You look good, too."

Kiana shrugged. "You're just being polite," she said, looking down at the same black slacks and gray button-up she had worn the day they met.

Genevieve smiled at her. "I'm just being honest," she said.

"I'm just trying to keep up," Kiana said, tugging on the cuffs of her shirt and grinning.

"Tell the truth, shame the devil, baby," Genevieve said with a sly smile.

Kiana cracked up. "Thank you for coming. I didn't know if you would. And if you did come, I imagined you'd only come to talk me out of it."

"You said you needed a friend. And since I'm the only friend you have down here, I had to come, right?" Genevieve said. "Especially since your other so-called friend is good for nothing. You had anything to drink?"

Kiana finger-picked her afro. "No," she lied. She swallowed a quick burst of bile in the back of her throat. "I need to do this clear-headed like I mentioned on the phone." Heat prickled at the base of her neck as she reconciled the two shots of Cuervo she had before she showered. A warm-up for someone like her. A small boost. And the hotel shot glasses were practically thimbles. Besides, the steam of the shower giving way to the moist cool of the late night air practically aerated the last of her buzz anyway.

"Good," Genevieve said. "The way you explained it, this closure is important. And when you get on your flight tomorrow…" She paused and placed her palm between Kiana's breasts. "You'll be well on your way to healing. You can find answers while you're up in the clouds and as close to the big man as we can get on this side of the dirt." She smiled with her mouth but not her eyes. They looked sad, a quick moisture shining in the strobe lights. She blinked and looked away.

Kiana swallowed hard. She took a deep breath and extended her arm. "Shall we?"

Genevieve nodded and tried another smile, this time her eyes played along. She linked her arm with Kiana's. "Let's go," she said.

They walked deeper into the dark club, past the dance floor where bodies undulated to the rapping snares and thumping bass drums. Couples of every combination clutched each other around the waist, pressed against each other's thighs, hips, and asses to music blasting from large overhead speakers, the sound raining down on them in torrents, their bodies soaked in sweat. Once past the main club area, they pushed through a heavy door with PRIVATE etched in the shiny wood surface. They entered a tight hallway, the walls lined with brass sconces and shadowboxes. The music hushed to a trembling throb. Looking at each other before glancing over their shoulders at the closing door behind them, they walked slowly toward another door at the end of the hall. A tall, buff white man with a chiseled face and spiked Billy Idol hair folded his bulging arms, his barrel chest nearly swallowing his clipboard. He looked at Kiana quickly, his eyes cold and green. He settled his eyes on Genevieve and his look softened, but only for a moment. The cold slickness came back, this time following the curves of Genevieve's body, so slow and arrant it could have left a slime.

"Excuse me," Kiana said. She stood up straight and squared her shoulders.

Genevieve shot her a look to stand down. Kiana wanted to ignore it, but she let Genevieve handle it. She reminded herself that Genevieve could take care of herself. She liked that about her, the sweetness that turned hard in an instant. Over the past few days, those shifts had been directed at Kiana, Genevieve going from an intriguing softness for her mouth to explore to a challenging toughness that threatened to crack her teeth. Kiana smiled.

Genevieve crossed her arms and cleared her throat. Her eyes narrowed and hardened. "Our names are on the list, not down the front of my dress," she said.

The man smirked and looked down at the clipboard. "Your names?" he said with a sigh.

Kiana still didn't like his tone. She wanted to snatch the clipboard from between his meaty paws and crack it over his bullet head. He must have felt Kiana's stare because he looked at her and twisted his lips in challenge. Kiana flexed her jaw and leaned forward. He shook his head dismissively and turned his attention to Genevieve, speaking directly to her and ignoring Kiana completely. "Your name?"

"It's her name you want," she said. Genevieve took a step back.

Kiana came forward. She slid her hands in her pockets. They trembled. She needed to break something. To drink something. The green-eyed bouncer infuriated her, the way he leered, the dismissive smirk on his thin, dry lips. Everything felt wrong. Her fingers ached inside her pockets. She curled them into fists. Tense and anxious, she looked to Genevieve for calm.

"My name is Kiana Lewis," she said. "I'm on the list with a plus one. This"—she reached her hand behind her and Genevieve took it—"is my plus one."

The man twisted his lips. "Yeah," he said, stepping away from the door. He unclasped the red velvet rope that stretched across the heavy wooden door, a gold plate etched with VIP in fancy script. He grabbed the long brass handle on the door and pulled it open. He rolled his eyes as Kiana gestured for Genevieve to go first.

"After you, baby," Kiana said. She threw a sidelong glance at the bouncer, who scoffed and crossed his massive arms across his clipboard. Genevieve smiled and walked through the door, pulling Kiana forward by reaching behind her and hooking her fingers onto the front of Kiana's pants.

Kiana smirked and raised an eyebrow at the bouncer. He sighed and turned away from them as they walked into the darkness beyond the door.

Once inside, the bar caught Kiana's eyes immediately. Long and taking up an entire wall, the clear, elegant glass bar glowed in the dark. Orange, red, yellow, and blue lights illuminated the bar from below, the colors dimming and giving way to each other in slow intervals as if taking cues from hypnotic rising and falling keyboards and electric guitar licks sliding around the room. Bottles lined the wall behind the bar, glasses of every shape and size hung overhead; the two bartenders, both dark-haired, olive-skinned women in tight black dresses, slid martini glasses and gimlets from the suspended racks with ease. There were no barstools, but a small group of blond-haired white women huddled at the far end of the bar, whispering to each other and sipping oversized glasses of blush wine. Opposite the bar, floor-to-ceiling two-way mirrors offered the VIP guests a view of the dance floor, bodies grinding and bumping to music only they could hear. Inside the VIP room, the mood was significantly more chill. The crisp air-conditioned air snapped at Kiana's skin as she looked around. A slow reggae groove eased about the room. Kiana could barely make it out. She listened, held her breath, and recognized Gregory Isaacs moaning to his night nurse, the longing faint but unmistakable.

Michelle's laughter rose up from a group of women seated on a large sectional. Her back to the door, the sound of her laugh, joyous and carefree, danced its way to where Kiana and Genevieve stood. Kiana stiffened. Genevieve found her hand and squeezed it.

One of the women, who sat next to a cinnamon-skinned woman with curious eyes and a wide mouth, lifted her face and smiled a tight-lipped smile in Kiana and Genevieve's direction. Carefree tendrils of copper hair framed her pale face, her sharp, straight nose and thin lips a contrast to the messy pile of hair curled on top of her head. Michelle turned around, a slight grin playing at the corners of her lips. She nodded at the women seated around her and walked over to Kiana and Genevieve.

"You came," she said. She held her arms open.

Kiana hugged her quickly, patting her on the back softly before pulling away. "I almost didn't," she said.

Michelle raised an eyebrow and glanced over at Genevieve. "You didn't respond to my text messages, but I'm sure you received my incentive," she said with a wink.

"Yeah," Kiana said. "I got it." She looked over at Genevieve with a small shrug.

"Well, I'm glad you're here," Michelle said. She smoothed the front of her dress, which was short and strapless, color-blocked gray and black spandex that fit her like a second skin.

Kiana took a deep breath. She found it difficult to look into Michelle's eyes. She needed to remember why she had come. She needed to forget the kiss from the other night. Yet, the glowing rainbow of a bar and enticing tug of the music threatened to pull her where she didn't want to go. Heat rose to her cheeks. Genevieve cleared her throat and squeezed Kiana's hand.

"I'm so fucking rude," Kiana said. She turned to Genevieve, hoping for an encouraging smile. Genevieve delivered. "This is my friend, Genevieve," she said.

Genevieve released Kiana's hand with a smile and extended her hand to Michelle, who looked down at it with a smug twist of lips. She chuckled and pulled Genevieve into an unexpected embrace.

"It's so nice to meet you," Michelle said. She pulled away from Genevieve, running her hands down her arms and holding her wrists. Her eyes traveled the length of Genevieve's body, lingering on her long, toned legs.

"Nice to meet you, too," Genevieve said, gently pulling her arms away from Michelle's grasp. She shot a confused look at Kiana.

"She's pretty," Michelle said to Kiana, her eyes still on Genevieve. "You like them pretty though. Pretty and easy."

"Excuse me?" Genevieve said. She put her hands on her hips.

"Oh, I didn't mean it like that," Michelle said. She placed a hand on her chest and laughed. "I meant friendly, easygoing, like that." She smiled. "I mean"—she turned to Kiana—"you've been here all of what? A few days?" She looked at both Kiana and Genevieve and said, "And here you both are. Friendly, cozy, and…" She shrugged and clapped her hands together. "Never mind."

"Yeah," Kiana said. "Never mind."

Genevieve raised an eyebrow and pursed her lips, her hands still on her hips, her head cocked on her shoulders.

"Let's go get a drink," Michelle said. She spun and headed toward the bar.

Kiana exhaled and reached out to massage Genevieve's shoulders. "See why I needed a friend?"

"Because your ex-girlfriend is a bitch?" Genevieve said. She relaxed under Kiana's fingertips. Her arms dropped to her sides. She smiled.

"She's just…" Kiana stopped and watched Michelle at the bar. She leaned on it, the light beneath the bar changing from red to orange, an inviting glow leading the way from her ankles and up her smooth, shapely legs, chasing away the shadows between her thick thighs. "She's just a little rough around the edges. Like you," Kiana said with a final caress along the nape of Genevieve's neck. She rested her hands on her shoulders.

Genevieve removed Kiana's hands from her body. "Baby, me and that character over there, ain't got nothing in common."

Kiana smiled. "Okay. I'm sorry if I saw a connection there. I like what I like," she said.

Genevieve raised her eyebrow in challenge, slapping at Kiana's shoulder.

"What?" Kiana chuckled. "Come on."

By the time they reached the bar, Michelle had already ordered three drinks.

"I know you don't like mixed drinks, Kiana," Michelle said, picking up one of the Collins glasses filled with what looked like dark, angry pink lemonade. She handed the drink to Kiana, who took it hesitantly. "Well, I know you don't *prefer* mixed drinks." She picked up another drink and held it out to Genevieve. "Truth is, Kiana's never met a drink she didn't like," she whispered in Genevieve's direction. She giggled. "Here. This one's yours."

Genevieve smiled a small, phony smile. "No, thank you. I don't drink."

Michelle's eyes widened, and she put the drink down on the bar, her mouth gaped open. She burst into raucous laughter. "Seriously?" She looked at Kiana.

Genevieve set her jaw on edge.

"Seriously," Kiana said. She turned to Genevieve. "I'll get you a cranberry juice." Genevieve smiled that same fake smile at Kiana, and her heart sank. Genevieve walked over to the opposite side of Kiana and leaned back on the bar, staring straight ahead. The woman with the carefree copper hair and razor sharp nose came up to Michelle, who composed herself by sipping from her drink.

"I'm surprised at you," Michelle said. The copper-haired woman whispered in her ear. "Excuse me a second," Michelle said. She and the woman took a step back and entered into a hushed conversation.

Kiana turned, raised her hand, and smiled as one of the bartenders came over to her right away. The woman licked her shapely, red-tinted lips and leaned on the bar, her breasts propped up against the rounded glass edge.

"And what can I do for you?" she asked. She bit at her bottom lip.

Kiana caught herself staring at the bartender's breasts, green and blue and yellow bouncing off the curve of them. She cleared her throat. "A cranberry juice. Can I get a cranberry juice? With a lime."

"That's no way to celebrate," the woman said.

Kiana looked over her shoulder at Genevieve who stared across the room at the two-way mirrors, watching the dance floor and nodding her head to the Portishead surging from the speakers above the bar. It suddenly felt like a mistake asking her to come with her. Or maybe it always felt like a mistake. She swallowed. The tequila long worn off, her throat felt dry and itchy. It ached. She unbuttoned another button on her shirt, the tension between Michelle and Genevieve choking her like a fishbone, a sharpness of anxiety just below her voice box. She swallowed again, forcing a smile.

"Can I just have the juice, please?" she managed to croak out.

The bartender curved her moist lips. "You can have anything you want, but we'll start with the juice." She licked her lips again before turning to get the juice. Kiana turned around, swiping up her drink but not sipping it. She stared into the glass. It smelled sweet.

"So you're on the wagon?" Michelle said, sliding closer to Kiana and talking across her. The copper-haired woman moved away from Michelle and leaned on the bar. She chatted with the bartender, both of them smiling and touching hands while they whispered.

Genevieve turned to Michelle but looked at Kiana, her eyes sending messages that made Kiana uncomfortable as she stood between them.

"I guess you can say that," Genevieve said.

Michelle laughed again, but not as heartily. She wrapped her lips around the narrow black straw of her drink and sucked. She reached out to take the straw from Kiana's drink. She tossed it on the bar, still sucking her drink. She glanced at Kiana and raised an eyebrow. She pulled her mouth off the straw and exhaled, her eyelashes fluttering.

"This shit is so fucking good," she said with a giggle. "I don't know how many I've had." She licked her lips. "So, you don't drink at all?" she said, shaking her head in confusion. She leaned on Kiana's shoulder.

"No, I don't." Genevieve frowned. "How many times do I need to say it?"

Michelle leaned back, a hand on her chest. "I'm sorry. Am I offending you? You don't have to be all sensitive and shit."

Genevieve shot a look to Kiana.

"Look, Michelle," Kiana began. She turned to put her drink down on the bar.

Michelle laughed again and nodded toward Kiana's abandoned cocktail. "You, too?" She sucked at her drink and laughed into her straw. "The pussy must be magic," she said, her teeth clenched on the tip of the straw.

"What the hell did you say?" Genevieve said, pushing herself off the edge of the bar.

Kiana turned to her, placing her hands on Genevieve's shoulders. "Genevieve, Genevieve," Kiana said, holding Genevieve still, turning to block her view of Michelle, who chuckled and stirred her drink.

Genevieve took her bottom lip between her teeth, her honey eyes glaring in the red to orange lighting of the bar. "You better get your girl," she said.

"I will," Kiana said. "I'm sorry. Just…" She stopped and took a deep breath, glancing over her shoulder over at Michelle. She frantically searched the bar for the woman with the beauty mark that was supposed to be getting Genevieve's cranberry juice. She spotted her still talking with the copper-haired woman. She turned to Genevieve. "Okay, I'm going to talk to her. She's drunk."

"I'm not drunk," Michelle said.

"Michelle, stop," Kiana said without turning to look at her. She squeezed Genevieve's shoulders and looked her in her eyes. "I'm going to talk to her. Then we'll go. Okay?"

Genevieve didn't say anything. She pursed her lips and rolled her eyes.

"Just go sit over there for me, please." Kiana jutted her chin toward a group of plush chairs surrounding a small glass table. The setup was opposite the sectional where Michelle's bridal party sat, talking and drinking. "I'll bring you your juice in a minute. Okay? Please."

Genevieve cut her eyes over Kiana's shoulder and clenched her jaw. She looked at Kiana with a sigh. "Ten minutes. You got ten minutes." She turned and walked over to the chairs.

"What the fuck is wrong with you, Michelle?"

Michelle laughed and sipped her drink. The straw slurped against the ice in the glass, the magenta liquor concoction nearly gone. "Nothing." She shrugged.

"Something's wrong with you," Kiana said. "You're being an asshole."

"Oh, really?" She smiled. "I wonder if it's the drinks?" She sucked down the last of her drink. "You think it might be the drinks?" She laughed.

Kiana turned away from her. The bartender finally brought the juice. She winked as she set it down. Kiana went into her pocket and took out a five.

"Open bar, baby," the woman said.

Kiana put the five on the bar anyway. The bartender looked at it, but didn't touch it. She smiled then stuck a wedge of lime on the edge of the short glass. "Enjoy." She nodded at Michelle, who set her empty glass down and nodded back to indicate a refill.

"You didn't even taste yours," Michelle said. She picked up Kiana's drink. The ice nearly melted, condensation dripped down the tall glass as she handed it to Kiana.

Kiana took it. Her mouth watered. "Michelle, I came here to tell you—"

"Just taste it," Michelle interrupted. She moved the glass toward Kiana's mouth. "Just one taste," she said. "Remember you used to say that to me? 'Just one taste'?" She leaned into

Kiana's side, her lips grazing her ear. "You used to slide your hand between my legs while I was sleeping. You would find my spot within seconds, and I'd get so wet."

Kiana's pussy clenched. She did remember. She would rub Michelle's hips and thighs while she slept. On the brink of sleep herself, Kiana teetered between haunting nightmares and waking dreams, caressing Michelle's smooth skin subconsciously but with an intention borne of unending desire. Her palm would find Michelle's pussy thick and hot, her fingers moving between the folds, more flesh, more heat. As Michelle groaned in halfhearted protest, Kiana would whisper her plea, *just one taste.*

Kiana took a deep breath as Michelle continued to whisper in her ear.

"I would let you," Michelle said. She chuckled softly. "Half-sleep but wanting you, I would let you. I would open for you. My legs would be limp with sleep, but then…" She sighed.

"Michelle, stop it," Kiana said. She shrugged Michelle off her shoulder and away from her ear. "I'll taste your drink, but cut the shit, all right?" She sipped the drink. Michelle knew her, knew that she didn't prefer mixed drinks, but she also knew what she liked when she had one. The drink's sweet smell was misleading. Kiana recognized whiskey instantly, the dry bite, then the sharp tang of lemon. She sipped again. A deep sip. She held the drink in her mouth, let it tingle on her tongue. She breathed through her nose, a faint berry sweetness, the snap of red wine.

"This is good," Kiana said. She drank more. "What is it?" She furrowed her eyebrows, sipping again, trying to figure it out for herself.

Michelle laughed. She pumped her fist. "Success!" she said. "I thought you would like it. I hoped you would." She giggled and picked up her new drink, the same deep pink, the same sweet smell. "It's called a Whiskey Seduction." She toyed with her straw, tapping it against her bottom lip.

Kiana took a few more sips then looked over at Genevieve, who sat cross-legged, looking out at the dance floor. Her foot bouncing with impatience. Kiana put her drink down. "The drink is good, but you are fucked up."

"Why?" Michelle sucked at her straw then put her drink down on the bar. She shrugged and tilted her head toward Genevieve. "Because of her?" She puffed air through her lips with a pout. "I was just messing with her," she said. "She can't take a joke? Then again, was it even a joke? The pussy must be good. She's so…I don't know…different. Odd." She scrunched her nose as she stared over at Genevieve. "I'm surprised by her. I'm surprised by you." She picked up her drink.

Kiana drank the last of hers but held on to the empty glass. The cold against her fingers felt comforting, almost as comforting as the whiskey which seemed to have settled her stomach, moistened her dry, aching throat.

"I would say I am surprised by you, but I guess I'm not," Kiana said.

"What do you mean?" Michelle asked.

"The kiss the other night. The tequila. The text message. 'Last night of freedom.' Even this fucking drink," Kiana said. She lifted her empty glass. "You're trying to get me. I know you. You're trying to use me. Even those things you said at the café. You could always manipulate my feelings." She shook her head. "Enough. I came to tell you I've had enough." She realized it as soon as she said it. Michelle did use her. She always knew how to turn things around, always made herself come out on top.

Michelle raised an eyebrow. She chuckled. "You came to tell me that *you've* had enough?" She licked her teeth and nodded. "And where did this epiphany come from? Her?" She tilted her drink toward Genevieve, who happened to look over at them in that very moment and crossed her arms in warning to Kiana.

"No," Kiana said. "Yes." She shook her head. "I don't know. I don't even know…"

"You're making too much of all of this," Michelle said. "I thought we were leaving all this shit in the past anyway. Didn't we agree to that?"

"Yeah, we did. Then you fucking kissed me. Then you sent me—"

"I sent you a celebratory drink. I designed a cocktail you would enjoy as you celebrated with me tonight. Is that a crime? To want to please my friend?" Michelle smiled. She sipped her drink then sighed. Her shoulders slumped. "You've had enough? Okay. Forget I even tried." She turned to the bar.

"No," Kiana said. "It's not like that." She faced Michelle and fought the urge to comfort her. She hated that she still cared so much. And for what?

"Am I feeling all nostalgic? Yes, I am. Maybe too nostalgic. But I'm fucking getting married. Married, Key." She turned to look at Kiana. Tears quivered at the rims of eyes, her silver eye shadow and black eyeliner elegant and seductive. "I'm scared." She shrugged.

Kiana put a hand on her shoulder. She looked up and the bartender caught her eyes. She smiled and licked her lips, raising her eyebrow with the eternal question. Kiana bit at the inside of her jaw.

Michelle dabbed at the corners of her eyes. "Look, I'm sorry. You know I'm a lightweight. I've been rude." She took a deep breath. She reached across Kiana and grabbed Genevieve's juice. "Let me take this over to your friend and apologize."

She smiled. "Maybe she'll agree to stay, and we can just party. Really celebrate the way we should. The way we need to." She put a hand on Kiana's arm and walked over to Genevieve.

Kiana watched Michelle as she carefully approached Genevieve. She sat beside her and handed her the juice. Genevieve took it. They began talking, Michelle using hand gestures, Genevieve nodding and sipping her juice. She turned back to the bar and nodded at the bartender, who smiled and grabbed a fresh Collins glass and the Maker's.

The bongos came first. Then the saxophone. Then Sade. "Smooth Operator." The copper-haired woman walked over to Kiana as if on cue. The bartender set a new Whiskey Seduction in front of Kiana and walked away. Kiana drew the glass nearer to her. She slid the straw from the glass and set it on the edge of the napkin under her drink. She picked up the cocktail, but before she could sip it, the copper-haired woman cleared her throat and leaned into her.

"I hope you're raising your glass for a toast," she said. She raised her drink.

Kiana toasted her own drink, lifting the glass but not clinking. She moved to drink.

"Tsk, tsk, tsk," the woman said. "You haven't said what we're drinking to."

Kiana shrugged. "Life," she said, raising her glass once more.

"To life," the woman said. "And love and liberty and freedom. Freedom most of all." She lifted her gimlet and clinked it against Kiana's glass. She giggled. "I didn't mean to clink. That's tacky right?" She drank from her glass and giggled.

"I guess," Kiana said. She drank deep swallows of the slightly sweet, mostly sharp mixture.

"I'm sorry," the woman said. "I've had A LOT of gimlets tonight." She laughed again. "My name is Evelyn." She extended her hand.

"I'm Kiana."

"Oh, I know who you are," Evelyn said. She sipped her vodka and raised her eyebrows while staring at Kiana over the rim of her glass. Her eyes were hazel with green flecks that glimmered every time the bar lights transitioned from yellow to orange. "You're a friend of Michelle's. A special friend." She giggled, the tip of her tongue flicking out to meet her top lip.

Kiana nodded. "I suppose you could say that." She looked over at the group of chairs. She didn't see Michelle or Genevieve. She searched the lounge, finally spotting Genevieve and Michelle standing among the women from the bridal party. Everyone stood in the center of the sectional, shaking hands and talking animatedly. She drank from her glass, feeling light-headed but heavy at the same time. She blinked slowly but drank quickly. She needed balance.

"I've heard a lot about you," Evelyn said.

"It's all lies," Kiana said, sipping from her glass.

Evelyn threw her head back and laughed. She put her gimlet on the bar and clapped her hands together once then folded them in front of her. Her skirt, a band of red leather that cut across her thin, pale white thighs, rode up as she lifted a leg up on the rail running along the bottom of the bar. "You don't even know what I've heard."

Kiana looked at Evelyn, really looked at her. Her sharp nose and deep-set eyes made her look severe, ravenous and exhausted at the same time. She tucked a curl behind her ear and adjusted the spaghetti strap of her black silk shirt, tiny sheer stripes exposing her red, strapless bra underneath.

"Was it good?" Kiana asked.

"Was what good?" Evelyn said, biting her lip.

"What you've heard."

"Yes," Evelyn said. She tilted her head in challenge.

"Then it's like I said," Kiana said. She sipped her drink and turned her attention to the sectional. Some of the women had been seated; others, Genevieve and Michelle included, remained standing. "All lies."

Evelyn chuckled. "Michelle was right about you. You are charming as fuck." She picked up her gimlet and drained the last of her drink. She motioned for the bartender. "Do a shot with me," she said, placing a warm hand on Kiana's arm. The heat radiated through the sleeve of her shirt.

"I really shouldn't," Kiana said. She pulled her arm away. She shook her drink, mixing the magenta drink with the clear, perfect cubes of ice in the glass.

"That won't get you very far in life," Evelyn said. "I should. I shouldn't. No fun in that."

Kiana smirked. The drink, which turned out to be a semi-sweet, beguiling mixture of whiskey, black currant liqueur, lemon juice, and red wine, went down quick and easy. She drained her glass and ordered another with a raise of her empty glass.

"Besides, it's usually the things that you shouldn't do that are the most fun," Evelyn said. She flipped a few errant curls out of her face, and when the bartender appeared, setting down another Whiskey Seduction for Kiana, she ordered two shots of Cuervo.

Kiana sipped her new drink and shifted toward Evelyn. "Cuervo?"

Evelyn smiled, her eyes shining in the yellow light. "I have it on good authority that tequila is a good choice for you."

"Nah, buddy, I don't really like tequila," Kiana said. She drank her cocktail, deep swallows that eased down her throat, soothing and smooth. She felt hands wrap themselves around her waist. A body pressing up on her from behind.

"That's not what we heard," a voice whispered into the nape of her neck.

Kiana spun around. The cinnamon-skinned woman with the big eyes and wide mouth smiled at her, still pressing forward.

"We're going to need another shot," Evelyn said.

"I'm Iman," the brown-skinned woman said, her breath hot against Kiana's face. The smell was familiar but unpleasant, menthol, burnt leaves. She rolled her body against Kiana's and planted a quick kiss beneath her ear.

"What the hell?" Kiana pushed her arms out, shoving Iman back. She stumbled then laughed.

"You need to loosen up," Iman said. "Evelyn, get them shots over here. And see if…you know…" She bucked her eyes at Evelyn, who, as if just remembering something, dug into the curly, messy pile of hair on her head and pulled out a tiny baggie filled with a small white tablets.

Kiana shook her head before Evelyn even offered. "I don't do drugs," she said. She reached out and grabbed Iman's wrists whose hands were constantly rubbing on Kiana's body.

"You are being a party pooper," Evelyn said. The bartender lined up two more shot glasses and poured them to the brim with tequila.

Iman scrunched her nose. "Cuervo?" She stuck out her tongue.

"Yeah, but it's 1800!" Evelyn said.

"True!" Iman said. She and Evelyn slapped hands and burst into laughter. They each grabbed a shot glass and looked at Kiana expectedly.

Kiana stared at the shots then looked at the two women. Iman, sensual and full in ways Evelyn was not, blew her a kiss.

Kiana shook her head. "I don't know what you two think you're doing, but—"

Iman cut her off by placing a slender finger across her lips. "Stop. Just stop." She leaned forward and kissed Kiana on the mouth without moving her finger.

"Tequila. Cuervo," Evelyn said. "Don't tell me you don't remember."

Kiana searched her brain, rifled through memories of parties past. Nothing came to her. She frowned, reaching across her body for her drink. She sipped it. The cool, dry whiskey charged with tart lemon, berries, and wine. Iman smiled at her and licked at the rim of her shot glass. Kiana thought of the tropical party on that cold Chicago winter's day, she and Michelle dancing to reggae in their underwear until, apartment chill be damned, their skin was slick with sweat. She drank again. She looked at Evelyn, her eyes glowing yellow, orange, then green. Her gaze fixed, her thin lips curled into a grin; she poked her tongue out. A single tablet sat on the tip of it; she flipped it into her mouth. Kiana looked away and set her drink down. She tried to look through the two women and find Genevieve. She needed Genevieve.

"I haven't been able to forget it since she told me about it," Iman said. Her hand caught Kiana's face, gripping it at her chin, short, sharp nails digging into her jaws.

"Apparently, you are quite good at what you do," Evelyn said.

"Good with plenty to go around." Iman smiled. Kiana gasped at the pinch of nails against her face. The nails scraped down to her chin. It hurt. She remembered.

Kiana's hair had been shorter then. Much shorter. Cropped close, small curls and tiny waves. Nails scratching at her scalp. Another pair of hands tugging at her pants. She wore button-fly jeans; the fingers moved deftly, unbuttoning one by one, slow and fast at the same time. Her T-shirt yanked up over her head. Her bra pushed off her breasts. She had reached up and found skin, hot, smooth skin. Michelle's thighs. She reached around. Michelle's ass. She had cupped it and pulled Michelle forward. Kiana had opened her eyes, shaved pussy inches from her nose. Michelle's. A moan. Someone else's. Michelle's mouth on her nipples. Someone else's mouth on her clit. Michelle's nails scratching across her stomach. Someone else's nails digging into her thighs. All of them too hard, too sharp. Pleasure halted by pain, slices and pricks against Kiana's skin like knives and needles. She didn't want it. She couldn't breathe.

Kiana's eyes burned at the flashes of memory; everything about it had felt wrong. She hadn't wanted it. She had told Michelle she didn't want it, not like that. Kiana looked frantically from Evelyn to Iman. She held her breath, unable to exhale, afraid of having to inhale. Drowning.

"I'm sure it wasn't 1800 then," Evelyn said.

"Two broke bitches on the South Side of Chicago?" Iman laughed. "I highly doubt it."

Iman and Evelyn slapped hands again, the tequila in their glasses sloshing over their fingers.

"We doing these shots or what?" Evelyn said. She lifted her glass. "What we drinking to?"

Iman stepped closer to Kiana, raising her glass, her menthol cigarette breath made Kiana gag.

"Get off me!" Kiana said, shoving Iman back.

"Don't be like that, Key," Evelyn said. She grabbed Kiana's arm.

"Yeah, Key," Iman said. "Don't be like that. Fuck, a toast then," she said. She threw her shot back and swallowed with a shiver that shook her braless breasts against the wrap of her silk dress.

"Don't call me that!" Kiana yelled.

"Oh, Key, relax," Evelyn said. "We're all friends here." She shot her tequila too, but instead of swallowing it, she held it in her mouth. She grabbed Kiana's face and smashed her thin lips against Kiana's. She stabbed her tongue into Kiana's mouth and pushed the tequila between her lips. The liquor, mixed with bitter chunks of Ecstasy, gurgled against their mouths and dripped down their chins. Iman laughed and moved closer to them both, her hand cupping Kiana's pussy through her pants before sliding around to her ass.

Kiana bucked both women off of her and spun around wildly to get free of them. Her arms swiped at the bar. Her glass of whiskey and Evelyn's gimlet crashed to the floor. The bartenders rushed over.

"Leave me the fuck alone!" Kiana said. "Get the fuck off me!"

"Key," Iman said, her face suddenly concerned. Evelyn doubled over in laughter.

"Don't call me that!"

Everyone stared at her. Genevieve and Michelle rushed over to her.

"Kiana, what happened?" Genevieve asked, trying to get close to her. Kiana pushed her away.

"Key, what's the problem? What happened?" Michelle asked. She glanced over her shoulder at her friends. "Evelyn? Iman? What the fuck?" Neither woman said anything. They shrugged and huddled together, linking arms and exchanging innocent looks.

"Key," Michelle said.

"FUCK YOU!" Kiana shouted. She whipped around and ran out of the lounge. She burst through the door so hard, she nearly knocked the bouncer over. He dropped his clipboard and grabbed Kiana by the collar of her shirt.

"What the fuck is wrong with you?" he said through clenched teeth. His green eyes cold and hard.

"Let me go!" Kiana yelled. She slapped at the bouncer's meaty hands then kneed him in the crotch.

"You little bitch!" he said, one hand flying to his crotch, the other catching Kiana around the neck.

By then the women from the VIP area had come to the door, holding it open and crowding around. Genevieve pushed her way through the collection of wide-eyed, drunk women.

"Let her go!" Genevieve said. She ran up on the bouncer and pulled on his forearm, trying to yank his hand from around Kiana's neck.

"Let her go, Sam," Michelle said, sliding between two women in black catsuits, chunky belts hanging low on their narrow hips. "Let her go!"

Sam cut his eyes at Michelle and grunted. He loosened his grip and backed away. Kiana crumpled to the floor, hacking and holding her neck. Tears streamed down her face, but she didn't wipe them. Genevieve knelt beside her. She rubbed her back.

"Come on," Genevieve whispered. "Stand up. Come on."

Genevieve helped Kiana to her feet. Kiana ran her arm roughly across her face. Her chest heaved. Her lips trembled. Her fists, clenched at her sides, throbbed against her thighs. She stared at Michelle. Michelle dropped her head then it lifted as if to speak. Kiana shook her head. There was nothing she could say, nothing Kiana wanted to hear. She imagined the sound of Michelle's voice making her ears bleed. Genevieve put an arm around her, and Kiana let her lead her out of the club.

## Chapter Fourteen

K iana sat at the desk. She glanced at the clock. It wasn't even midnight. She stared at the bottle of Cuervo and swallowed the acidic bubbles that repeatedly rose in the back of her throat. Her eyes burned. She had cried all the way to the hotel, silent tears rolling down her face, Genevieve holding her hand in the cab, also silent. Now she sat on the bed, gripping the edge of the mattress, staring at her bare feet, her silver stilettos leaning against each other near the door.

The bottle of tequila was practically full. The couple of shots Kiana had before she left for the club hadn't put a dent in the bottle. Her eyes went from the empty glasses to the sliced lime, from the sliced lime to the bottle. Tears stung her eyes; she blinked and they fell. She ran her hands over her hair, finally resting her head in her hands. She sobbed.

"What happened, Kiana?" Genevieve asked. She didn't move from the bed, only leaned forward, her eyes soft and mouth turned down. She looked worried and uncertain.

Kiana blew out a loud, heavy breath. She sniffled and wiped at her face, drying her hands in the bunches of curls and naps at the top her head. She reached for the bottle of tequila.

"Kiana, don't," Genevieve said.

Kiana squared her jaw. She gripped the bottle and stood. She held it, stared down at it, then whipped it against the wall. Genevieve gasped. The bottle burst, bits of glass flying and golden liquor running down the wall.

"There's so much I don't remember, Genevieve," Kiana said. "So much I don't remember that I should remember." She dropped into the desk chair. She leaned back and stared at the wall where the bottle had burst. The stain like a Rorschach. Kiana saw a million images, a billion shapes. Faces and bottles, hearts and houses, clouds and hands.

"We block out the things that hurt us the most. And depending on what we use to do the blocking, we throw the baby out with the bath water," Genevieve said. She looked at Kiana, concern showing itself in her light eyes.

Kiana shook her head. "Mrs. Joyce, the woman who raised me and my sister, if you want to call it that, told me that my mama was a dope fiend. I asked her about my mama, and that is what she told me. She said she was a good-for-nothing junkie that died of an overdose in front of her babies." She wiped at her eyes. "I called her a liar and she slapped me. I told Karyn what happened, what that fat old bitch said, and she hugged me so tight." Kiana smiled through the pain. "She hugged me and told me that the old fat bitch was a liar and that our mama wasn't no dope fiend."

Genevieve watched Kiana from where she sat. She slid her hands under her thighs.

"Later, shit, I had to have been thirteen, I asked Karyn what mama died from. And I was already a mess at that point. Drinking, skipping school, and running through best friends based on whether or not they would let me finger them." Kiana chuckled without a trace of humor. "Anyway, Karyn came to pick me up from Rainbow Beach. I was damn near drunk off

Boone's, my drink of choice at the time. I asked her about how mama died while we walked to the bus stop. She lied to me about it. She told me she died in her sleep, an aneurism or some shit. I didn't even know what the hell that was."

"How did you know it was a lie?" Genevieve asked.

"Because I remembered seeing her. I remembered seeing my mama on the floor, convulsing or something, I don't know. But it wasn't in her sleep. I remember seeing her on the living room floor, shaking, and my sister pushing me back into the kitchen. For a while, when I was way young, I used to tell myself it was a dream. I would wait for her to come get us from Mrs. Joyce's house. Shit, I hated her old fat ass, and she didn't like me, so I just prayed and wished and hoped all the time for my mama to come get me. When she never came, I knew then that seeing her on the floor like that wasn't a dream. It wasn't even a nightmare. It was a memory. My last memory of my mama." Kiana stood. She fidgeted with her shirt, which she had pulled out from her pants. She unbuttoned her cuffs and rolled the sleeves up to her elbows. She felt Genevieve's eyes on her.

"I drank to forget it. Drinking was the only way to forget it. It was the only thing I could trust. When my sister lied to me on the way to the 87th street bus, I knew I could never fully trust her either."

"She was trying to protect you, Kiana," Genevieve said.

Kiana shook her head. She pushed the empty buckets aside and reached behind the lamp. The bottle of Southern Comfort was warm and heavy in her hand. She licked her lips and twisted off the small black cap. Her back to Genevieve, she slowly brought the bottle to her lips. Shame burned under her eyes, and she felt tears building. She took a deep breath.

"Kiana, what are you doing?"

Kiana glanced over her shoulder, panting, lips quivering. Genevieve pushed herself up from the bed, sidestepping the broken glass and wet carpet near the nightstand. She crept closer to Kiana, holding her hands up as if Kiana had a gun.

"Kiana, don't. You don't need to do that."

Kiana bit the inside of her cheek and turned away from Genevieve. She brought the bottle to her lips and drank, eyes closed and throat gulping.

"Damn it, Kiana!" Genevieve yelled. She pushed Kiana in the back.

Kiana lurched forward. She caught herself on the back of the desk chair. It leaned back and swiveled. Kiana lost her balance and fell to the floor. The bottle snapped from her lips, hit the carpet, and started to roll beneath the bed. Kiana caught it. She balanced herself and sat up, planting the bottle between her legs. She leaned on the neck of the bottle. She struggled to catch her breath from the hungry gulping and the shock of the fall.

"You don't get to do this," Genevieve said. She walked around the foot of the bed to face Kiana, who sat on the floor, cross-legged in front of the windows.

"Do what?" Kiana said.

"This…" She held her hand out, gesturing at Kiana and the bottle of Southern Comfort between her legs like a post. "Tell me these things. Burst open and rain down all this sorrow and pain and…you don't get to drown me in your tragic stories."

Kiana looked at Genevieve, incredulous. "But this is what you wanted. You wanted me to crack open. I can talk in poems, too. Metaphors and shit. All you've been doing is trying to bust me open like some overstuffed bag of garbage, so you could clean up the mess. Well, here I am, V, clean me up."

Genevieve blinked back her tears. She bit her lip and turned away from Kiana. "That's not what I've been doing," she said.

"Well, what have you been doing?"

Genevieve shrugged but didn't turn around.

"Figures," Kiana said. "Leave me the fuck alone then. I'm always alone anyway. I should be used to it by now." She lifted the bottle of Southern Comfort and guzzled from it. The liquor, warm and thick and sweet, coated her throat, slowly rolling down to the very core of her, a fire pit growing in her belly.

"You're not alone," Genevieve said. She faced Kiana, looked down at her. "You've got people who care about you. You've got your sister. You've got...you've got me." She put her hands on her hips. "Regardless of how you've treated me, and even against my own best judgment, I've been with you."

Kiana laughed. She swigged from the bottle. "You haven't been *with* me, V. You've been hovering over me," she said. She didn't know why she used Genevieve's nickname; it just came out. She recalled that first morning she woke up in Genevieve's apartment. *My friends call me "V,"* she had said. Kiana swallowed. Is that what they were? Friends? She shook her head, confusion mounting. She almost lost her train of thought. "You've been hovering. Looking down at me like I'm some kind of traffic jam or car crash."

Genevieve knelt on the floor but kept her distance. Her eyes darted from the bottle of SoCo to Kiana and back again. "That's not how I've tried to be, Kiana. I was broken just like you once, baby. A billion pieces, jagged pieces that cut me, sliced me on the regular, but I—"

Kiana cut her off. "Your smug little smile and all your lame ass sayings about faith and love and survival and all that other bullshit that don't mean nothing to me right now..." She struggled to continue, her voice bitter and hard. "...and your pity. Your fucking pity." Her face cracked, the tears came. "I don't need it. I don't need it from Michelle. I don't need it from

Karyn. I don't need it from you. I need...I need someone to come close. I'm so tired of being alone," she choked out the words. "I'm...so...tired...of...being..."

Genevieve crawled forward. She slid the bottle of liquor from Kiana's hands. She sat, holding the Southern Comfort with both hands. Kiana cried still, her body slumped forward in the absence of the bottle's stability. Her shoulders shook as she cried. Genevieve stared at the bottle; she licked her lips and took a deep breath. Kiana choked on a sob and looked up at Genevieve. Their eyes locked. Their chests heaved with the same labored breathing. Neither one of them blinked; neither one of them moved.

Kiana couldn't read Genevieve's mind, but she didn't have to. She looked into Genevieve's honey eyes, the desperate way she clutched the bottle, and she knew everything there was to feel: Fear. Loneliness. Confusion. Disappointment. Hope. Need. Desire. Exhaustion. A list of feelings on one hand, yet just words on the other. Words that could be spoken or not, written or erased. They were meaningless. It all was. Everything meant nothing.

Kiana closed her mouth and held her breath. She reached out her hand, but it seemed to move in slow motion, her arm aching as she pushed through layers of time, of memory and pain. Genevieve brought the bottle to her lips, just beyond the reach of Kiana's fingertips. She took one sip. A small one.

Kiana gasped. She knew it for sure now, and she knew that Genevieve knew it, too.

Nothing mattered.

The burden of knowledge pressed down on both of them, and Kiana understood that coming together was the only way to keep from being crushed into oblivion. She pushed through the thickness of the air between them. She snatched the bottle from

Genevieve, but Genevieve snatched it back. She drank from it, the thick amber liquor seeping out the corners of her mouth, snaking down her neck. Kiana swiped at the bottle again, yanking it from Genevieve's grasp.

They tussled for control of the bottle. It shook and twisted and turned between them, Southern Comfort splashing up from inside, splattering across their faces until Kiana gripped it from the bottom. The bottle tilted, and the liquor poured out onto Genevieve's chest, drizzling between her breasts and staining the front of her dress. Genevieve snatched the bottle and tossed it behind her. Kiana dove onto her tongue first, her mouth sucking at Genevieve's neck and shoulders, tongue lapping at the mounds of her cleavage.

Kiana pushed Genevieve's dress up her hot thighs. Genevieve opened her legs wide to welcome Kiana between them. They kissed, sucking the liquor off each other's tongues and licking each other's lips. Genevieve pulled at Kiana's shirt, buttons popping off in the effort. Kiana hurriedly unbuttoned the ones that remained and shrugged the shirt off her shoulders. She reached down and pressed her hand against Genevieve's pussy. It throbbed against her palm. She moved her thong aside and dipped her fingers inside.

Genevieve didn't stop her this time. She reached above her head and searched for the bottle of Southern Comfort. When she finally gripped it, she brought it to her face, sitting up to drink. Kiana paused her exploring fingers and watched her. The muscles trembling in her stomach, the vein pulsing in her neck. Kiana took the bottle from her and sipped from it, her fingers slick and sticky around the neck of the bottle. On her knees, chest heaving while she drank, she watched Genevieve sit up completely and pull her dress over her head. She flung it away, her bare breasts rounded and full. She pulled at the front of

Kiana's pants, and she scooted forward on her knees. The last of the Southern Comfort sloshed around the bottom of the bottle.

Kiana bent down to kiss Genevieve, the remnants of the liquor warm and sweet on their tongues. Kiana grabbed Genevieve's hair, jerked her head back, and held it tilted, the length of her neck stretching, her breasts pointed up from the deep arching of her back. Kiana took another sip of booze before gripping near the mouth of the bottle and slanting it sideways over Genevieve's neck and chest. She poured Southern Comfort between Genevieve's breasts, watching the thick amber liquid slowly drip down in crooked lines that rolled over Genevieve's heaving breasts and quivering stomach, the muscles showing themselves in each panting breath.

Kiana licked her lips and poured more. Southern Comfort, velvet smooth, found the curves of Genevieve's breasts, dripped from her rigid nipples. When the bottle was near empty, Kiana shook it, holding it by the bottom, drops spattering Genevieve's lips and chin. She opened her mouth and stuck out her tongue like trying to catch raindrops. A last errant drop landed on her forehead like an anointing.

Kiana dove in, sucking the liquor from Genevieve's skin, her tongue licking and lapping, her lips kissing and teeth biting. Genevieve moaned from somewhere deep inside her, the sound carnal and wild in Kiana's ears. Kiana matched the noise; she sighed and moaned, cried and whimpered as Genevieve gave herself, gave all of herself. In the darkness of it all, the carpet burning knees and elbows, the air moist with sweat and liquor and tears, fingers pumping and aching, nails scratching and teeth biting, Kiana and Genevieve found each other, crashed into each other.

When Kiana finally buried her face between Genevieve's thighs, she discovered a sweetness, a thickness, an intoxication that rivaled any drink she'd ever had. Genevieve twisted and turned against Kiana's mouth. Kiana, light-headed and dizzy with pleasure, smothered herself in the depth of Genevieve, losing her breath but continuing, suffocating but welcoming the terror, drowning, dying, but not caring at all.

Genevieve burst with a rush of wet that Kiana desperately swallowed, the waves of the climax matching her own. She cracked open, shattering into a million pieces, her own wetness soaking the carpet beneath her trembling thighs.

Kiana rolled onto her back. She looked up at the window and around the room. Moonlight poured into the darkness of the room and reflected a pale, disappointed light on the empty bottle of Southern Comfort and the pile of sweaty sorrow that was her and Genevieve, their bodies intertwined, their legs and arms a tangled, limp mess.

# CHAPTER FIFTEEN

*Saturday*

Kiana's head crashed like cymbals when she opened her eyes. She forced herself to sit up. The room was bright with morning sun and musty with the smell of sweat and booze. Confused, she searched the room for answers, for clues, to what, she didn't quite know. She looked down at herself, naked and sticky. She panicked. Her mind went from blank slate to flashing faces, yellow-eyed Medusas and spiky-haired demons. She closed her eyes, squeezed them so tight it hurt her face. The darkness swirled behind her eyes, the bed floating on a river of blood.

She opened her eyes, darkness prevailing, flames curling up around the edges of the mattress. A hand shot up from beside the bed, grabbing her, her thigh burning from the touch. She swatted it away. Genevieve's voice. Inaudible whispers. Michelle's laughter, rising up and shaking the entire room, the rumble of it cracking the furniture, shattering the windows, and crumbling the walls. Genevieve, covered in blood, appeared at the foot of the bed and crawled toward her on all fours, screaming her name, her voice like sirens.

Kiana opened her eyes and sat up, panting, the pain in her head like crashing cymbals, the air stale with sweat and the funk of wet carpet. She wiped at her face, her fingers aching and sticky. She looked around the empty room and down at the bed, down at herself. The bed was a twisted collection of crumpled sheets, stiff and stained in places. Her breasts were bare with red splotches and teeth marks along the heft of them, around her dark, puckered nipples.

Glass shards littered the bedside table; a brown inkblot blossomed from a dent in the wall above the lamp. Her eyes burned as she surveyed the room, fear bubbling up from the pit of her stomach. Something rose up, something foul and sour. Her teeth chattered, and the walls of her mouth watered, the saliva warm and bitter. Kiana's face flushed, sweat beaded at her temples, and something grew inside her, full of gas and bile, something expanding into her chest, burning and churning, yet pushing up solid and persistent.

She turned her head to the side of the bed just in time.

A belch of vomit exploded from her stomach, shredded gray chunks and spongy clumps of pink, burnt orange slime swirled in thick, liquid brown. She gagged at the smell of it, the sight of it. Heaving and yacking again, elastic strings of spit with red-tinted bubbles hung from her trembling lips to the stinking pile of vomit on the floor, the splatters on the base of the nightstand. Her face on fire, tears stinging her eyes, and stomach lurching, she collapsed over the side of the bed, slipping in her own refuse.

She pushed herself up, naked and weak, half-crawling, half-walking toward the bathroom, her hands and arms slick with sweat and vomit. It came again, an acidic balloon of sour, expanding in her stomach and pushing up her ribcage, pushing apart the bones, swallowing her breath. She wretched, and a trembling hand flew to her mouth, covering it. She tried in vain to hold it, but the putrid mixture erupted from her throat and burst through her fingers and shot out her nose, spraying into the air and dripping down her arm. Vomit burned her tongue and the inside of her nostrils.

Horrified and choking, she tried to run. Her foot kicked at an empty bottle; her ankle caught on her discarded pants. Her arms flailed as she pitched forward and barreled toward the half-closed door of the bathroom, the force of her trip pushing it open.

The door slammed against the sink, and Kiana hit the cool tile of the bathroom floor. She belched again, a bubble of acrid spit bursting at her lips. The floor, solid and cold, calmed her frantic heartbeat and chilled her burning skin. She slept.

## CHAPTER SIXTEEN

Kiana's phone sat silently on the nightstand. Kiana stared at it as if in a trance, as if she could will it to ring. She glanced at the clock. It had been two hours since the cleaning woman had found her, snoring in a pool of her own vomit on the bathroom floor.

The woman, sepia-skinned with dark eyes, cursed in French as she had run Kiana a bath. She had gently helped her into the tub, muttering under her breath. While Kiana soaked, silent and beyond ashamed, the woman had cleaned the room—the vomit and broken glass, the strewn clothes and soiled sheets. Kiana, afraid to close her eyes, stared straight ahead at the light green tile and timed her breathing to the fat, slow bulbs of water that dripped from the bathtub faucet. The sound of the door slamming had jolted her from her trance, and she jumped up from the tepid water. She yanked open the bathroom door, and though naked and dripping with water, she rushed to the desk and side table, finally finding her wallet.

She snatched all the cash she had left and ran to the door. She opened it and spotted the woman walking down the hall, cartwheels squealing. Kiana called out to her; the woman didn't turn. She made it to the elevators. Kiana had called out to her again, wanting to thank her, wanting to give her money, but the woman hadn't turned around. She simply crossed herself quickly, the same gesture Genevieve made at the passing ambulance, and pushed her cart into the elevator.

Thinking of Genevieve snapped her back to the present. She put her hand on her phone and pulled it back. Kiana smoothed the front of her T-shirt and drummed her fingers against her thighs, never taking her eyes off her phone. *Ring. Ring. Ring.* She reached for it again, then stopped. She returned her hands to her jeans, rubbing her palms against them until they were warm. She couldn't call again. She shouldn't. Ten times would be considered crazy and obsessive, so she had no concept of what the twenty calls she had made to Genevieve in the past two hours would be considered.

Her head ached, a dull throb at the base of her skull. She scratched at her scalp then bit at the inside of her cheek. She glanced across the room at the desk. Her flask lay on its side, a glint of sunlight catching the curved bottom. She swallowed against a tickling itch at the back of throat. She grabbed her phone and left the room.

The hotel lobby was busy. Families in small huddles of antsy children and bored adults, inching forward in lines, checking in and checking out. Kiana glanced over her shoulder at the bar. The bartender, an unfamiliar face with pale white skin and yellow blond hair, nodded hello in her direction while drying glasses with a white towel. She forced a smile and walked quickly toward the glass doors, rushing out to the street as if being chased. Her phone rang, vibrating against her ass. She yanked it out of her back pocket, praying it was Genevieve.

"Hi, Karyn," Kiana said. Her throat hurt from throwing up all morning. It sounded like she'd eaten a bowl of gravel for breakfast.

"You sound terrible," Karyn said.

"I know. I feel terrible." Kiana looked up and down the street, automatically eyeing the liquor store. A woman carrying a purse and cloth grocery bag struggled with her purchases, three bottle necks clearing the top of the brown paper bag, and scurried to a waiting cab. Kiana turned away from the liquor store and walked in the opposite direction.

"I thought you were coming home. I waited for you to call with flight information. I called you. I'm trying to let you figure this thing out for yourself, but—"

"I miss you," Kiana interrupted. She meant to apologize, but it felt wrong and obvious. Of course, she was sorry; she had been sorry for years. Silence met her declaration. "Karyn? Are you there?"

Karyn cleared her throat. A door creaked and snapped shut. She had gone out to the front porch. Kiana closed her eyes for a moment, seeing her. Karyn was beautiful. Graceful and tall, serious and caring. She saw her walking toward the top step of the cement porch, no shoes, her toes, painted bright red or coral pink, curled over the edge. A breeze blew, Kiana heard it rustle against the receiver, and she imagined it catching Karyn's hair, sandy brown and straightened, a few strands escaped from her ponytail and sailing in the wind.

"I'm here," Karyn said. "I miss you, too."

Kiana took a deep breath. She walked along the street, moving through throngs of tourists and sliding past tables covered in beaded souvenirs and T-shirts, bootleg CDs and handcrafted incense holders. "I'm tired of apologizing," she said. A streetcar whirred past, and Kiana felt it in her teeth. Her head pounded and jaws ached.

"What did you say? Kiana, I can't hear you," Karyn said.

"I said, I'm tired of apologizing." Kiana cupped her hand around the bottom of her cell phone, trying to block out the street noise. "I'm tired of apologizing, and I can only imagine how tired you are of hearing me do it."

"Where is all this coming from? Are you all right?" Karyn's voice rose in pitch. The wind blew again, covering her voice with whooshes and whistles.

"I'll call you back," Kiana said. She stopped at the crosswalk and searched up and down the street. She looked up; she had walked to the river.

"No! Don't go!" Karyn said. She heard the creak of the screen door, the clack of it closing behind her. "Kiana, you're scaring me. Kiana?"

"Yeah," Kiana said. "I've got to go." She crossed the street as the walk signal lit up, a rush of Asian tourists snapping random pictures crowding her as she walked.

"Don't. Kiana, talk to me," Karyn said, her voice sounded desperate.

"Karyn?" Kiana stopped at the entrance to the Riverwalk.

"Yes?"

"How do you do it? How do you make it?" Kiana continued into the park, walking across the path and grass, stopping at the rocks near the bank.

"What?" Karyn asked. "How do I make what? What are you talking about? Look, just come home. Come home today. Whatever the time. Whatever the cost."

"How do you make it without Mama?" Kiana said. "I miss her. I miss her all the time." Her voice cracked. The pressure of holding back her tears squeezed at her brain, her head about to explode.

"Kiana? Why are you asking me that?" Karyn said. Her voice trembled with uncertainty and fear. "Just come home. We'll talk all about it. Me and you. We'll figure it out."

The tears fell. The crushing pain in Kiana's head intensified, a sharp pain like lightning flashed across the top of her head. "I didn't even know her, Karyn. I didn't even know her, and I miss her so much. You knew her! You got the chance to know her! How do you make it with her gone? How do you—"

"SHE'S NOT GONE!" Karyn screamed into the phone.

"What?" Kiana said, choking on tears and snot. "What do you mean? She's dead. I saw her. Don't lie to me again. She's dead, Karyn. She's gone."

"Not to me," Karyn said softly. "She's not gone. In my mind, in my heart, she is here." Her voice echoed against the empty house; Kiana pictured her on the sofa, the only furniture besides a second-hand coffee table in the middle of the front room. She clutched the phone with one hand, the other hand holding her head, her palm pressed against her forehead. It was the way Karyn always sat when she talked about serious things, painful things. Kiana saw it clearly, the wide open space of the front room where she had been chastised and lectured— skipping school, stealing candy, kissing girls, and drinking. She had helped Karyn finally clear out all of Mrs. Joyce's things only a year ago, and had promised to help her redecorate, another promise broken.

"She's not gone," Karyn repeated. "She died, but she's still here. She's always here. She's here for me, and for you, Kiana."

Kiana cried into the phone. A few passersby screwed their faces at her, but she didn't care. She folded herself down, squatting slowly before plopping onto the flat top of a large, jagged rock. She looked out at the muddy river, her vision blurred by tears, the smell of dirt and rain accenting her deep sobs.

"Come home," Karyn said. "Please come home."

"I will," Kiana said. She slid the phone from her ear and wiped her eyes with the back of her hand.

## CHAPTER SEVENTEEN

The hotel had simmered down, but not by much. Full tables of clacking silverware and clinking glasses replaced the lines snaking to and from the front desk. Kiana walked across the lobby with her hands stuffed in the pockets of her jeans. The bar beckoned. She couldn't deny it. She wanted a drink. Yet, she didn't want a drink. It was a strange feeling. Her mouth watered and muscles tensed as she passed the bar, trying not to look at the bottles lining the back wall, trying not to stare into the faces of the people who sipped happily on cocktails and chugged joyfully on beers.

Kiana paused at the elevator, debating. Her head needed quiet. A drink would quiet the painful throbbing. A drink would quiet the voices—Karyn's voice, Genevieve's voice, her own voice. But as much as she yearned for the numbing silence of it all, she needed to hear what the voices had to say. She may have wanted a drink, but she needed to listen. She took out her phone and scrolled to Genevieve's number. She pushed the button for the elevator then pressed "send" to call Genevieve for the twenty-first time. Straight to voice mail. She ended the call without leaving a message, and staring down at Genevieve's blinking name and number, she debated calling again.

"Kiana!" a voice boomed across the lobby. She looked up from her phone. Michelle's fiancé, Michael, came bounding up the hall. Random strands of hair stuck straight up from his frizzy, unbrushed waves, and a shadow of coarse hair covered his cheeks and chin. "Kiana! I need to talk to you!"

The elevator door opened with a ding. Kiana slid her phone into her pocket and sighed. Michael's eyes, puffy, red, and wild, crinkled in relief when Kiana let the elevator door close without stepping inside.

"Thank you. Thank you," he said. He reached out to her then corrected himself when Kiana pulled back.

"What do you want?" Kiana said. She glanced over at the bar.

"Have you..." he began, his voice wavering. He cleared his throat and ran a hand over his scruffy hair. "Have you seen Michelle? I can't...I can't find her. No one has heard from her."

"No, I haven't," Kiana said. "How long has she been missing?"

"Since her party. No one has heard from her since the party."

Kiana looked away. A flash of memory. Michelle's lips grazing her ear. *Just one taste.* Deep pink drinks. Breath like menthol cigarettes. Pills.

"No," she said again. "I haven't seen her."

Michael's body slumped. Being so tall, the gesture seemed exaggerated. It was odd seeing him so lanky and weak. His charcoal gray slacks looked dull, and the wrinkles in his untucked undershirt made it look like he had just tumbled from bed. Kiana remembered the first time she saw him. Met him. Confident and sure, his smile and his eyes full of satisfaction, his neat hair, smooth face, and tailored suit, exuding success.

"It's just that no one has heard from her. No one knows where she is." He clasped his hands together, his long fingers locking as if in prayer. "Please, if you know something. Anything." His eyes begged Kiana to allay his worst fears.

Kiana tried to imagine exactly what that meant. What were his worst fears? That Michelle was hurt or that she was upstairs?

"I swear to you. I haven't seen her since the party, and I don't know where she is," Kiana said.

"But you were at the party? So you were with her there?" Michael searched Kiana's eyes, staring into them deeply.

"Michael, what are you doing here?" Kiana said. "What do you want?"

"I know, all right?" he said.

"You know what?" Kiana shrugged. Her mind plagued with darkness when she tried to recall the details of the night, she tried to push past the alcoholic haze.

"I know you used to fuck my fiancée!" Michael raised his voice, walking up on Kiana. A few people from the dining room turned their heads. The bartender stopped rattling the shaker and frowned in their direction.

Kiana swallowed hard. Her fists clenched at her sides, her shoulders squared. "So what? Yeah, I used to be involved with Michelle, but that's over. It's been over."

"I'm not stupid." His lips snarled over his straight, white teeth. "You're still in love with her."

"No. I'm not," Kiana said with a certainty that surprised her. It was the truth, as real as gravity. The time she spent with Michelle in the past was a high, the excitement of finding someone who accepted her as is lifted her up. Yet in reality, being with Michelle was just like drinking. The high, the intoxication, the feeling of weightlessness. It was all temporary. It never lasted. Kiana always came crashing down, hurting herself and everyone around her more and more each time.

"I'm not in love with her," she said again.

"Prove it," Michael said. He looked like he wanted to punch her, like maybe he wanted to grab her around the neck and choke her.

Kiana's hand traveled slowly to her chest, her fingers moving up to her neck. The bouncer had choked her outside the VIP. She had almost forgotten. She swallowed again, the soreness in her throat suddenly more than acid burn from vomiting. What else happened last night? Genevieve helped her with the bouncer, had been with her after. Why didn't she take her calls?

"Prove it? You sound ridiculous. How the hell can I prove it?" Kiana said.

"Help me find her," Michael said.

## CHAPTER EIGHTEEN

K iana shouldn't have agreed. She went bar to bar, hotel to hotel in the Quarter, Michael nearby. He checked upstairs while she checked downstairs; he searched inside lounges while she searched outside patios. They made their way to Jackson Square, the throngs of tourists posing in front of the Jackson statue, the steed rearing up in triumph. Kiana dipped into gift shops and cafés; Michael called out Michelle's name on crowded corners.

"This is stupid," Kiana said. She leaned against a storefront catching her breath.

"It's not stupid," Michael said. He took out his phone and called Michelle's cell. "Still straight to fucking voice mail." He kicked at a small display of New Orleans postcards and key chains. It shook and rattled. Kiana reached out to steady it. "Did you try calling her?" Michael asked.

"No. You said her phone is going straight to voice mail, so calling wouldn't make a difference." She shrugged and thought of Genevieve. Her phone, too, kept going to voice mail. Kiana thought about her calls not even registering, going unnoticed, unmissed. She bit at the inside of her cheek, trying to remember more of what happened after the party.

"Where do you want to look next?" Michael said. He spit into the street. The action seemed dirty and common. The search had deflated him, brought him low. He had been bright and shiny when Kiana first met him, now he looked tired and dull. The light gone from his eyes. The charm vanished from his voice. Kiana felt sorry for him, yet exhaustion and the stress of her own miseries had gotten the best of her.

"Michael, I'm really sorry Michelle is missing," Kiana said. "Maybe she's just nervous about the wedding tomorrow. Brides get cold feet, too, right?" She forced a smile that Michael didn't return. "You should go back to the hotel. She's probably already there."

"She's not there. She would call." He spoke through clenched teeth, his jaws tight.

Kiana sighed. She looked up and down the street. She shook her head. "Just go back to the hotel. I'm sure she'll call you. She'll come back."

Michael started to speak, but his voice caught. He cleared his throat and spit again. "Let's check the French Market then come back by the café one more time." He reached out a hand. Kiana didn't pull back. Michael squeezed her arm. "Please," he said, his eyes watering.

Kiana agreed. She and Michael walked around the market. She weaved in and out the crowds sifting through scarves and hats, trying on sunglasses and jewelry, tasting hot sauces and seasonings. She met up with Michael at a small fountain, a painting of the French Market framed in brilliant blue as the backdrop, a statue of a woman, small breasts and full thighs reclining in satisfaction. Kiana shook her head in defeat, and she and Michael walked back toward Café Du Monde.

At the café, the usual swarms of tourists shuffled between the tables, the smell of sugar and roasted coffee thick as smoke.

Kiana scanned the tables and line; pigeons cooed and fluttered about as she circled the seating area. She walked from one side to the other, finally stopping outside the green covered dining area. She walked away from the café and rested against a small railing near a bench and light post. Palm bushes rustled in the breeze. She took out her phone. She put it back. She took it out again. She wanted to call Genevieve again. She had to keep trying. The loud, rolling growl of a Harley startled her. She pushed herself off the gate and turned to face the street.

Taz, her platinum hair unmistakable, her body just as big and broad as Kiana remembered, twisted the throttle on her bike, bluish gray smoke curling out the twin chrome pipes on either side of the thick rear tire. Kiana scanned the sidewalk, peered through people strolling up the street and pouring in and out of the café. A man, spray-painted to look like shiny metal, set up a boom box and wooden platform right in front of her. She rushed past him, almost knocking him over, paint smudging her arm and T-shirt. The motorcycle revved once more. Then, Genevieve. She looked sad. In a simple white T-shirt and skinny jeans, she looked small. She clutched a small white bag from the café and made her way to Taz's Harley.

Kiana ran up to her, grabbing Genevieve's arm before she could swing her leg over the back of the rumbling motorcycle. Genevieve reared back, yanking her arm from Kiana's grip.

"Get the fuck away from me," Genevieve said.

"Why? Why won't you talk to me?" Kiana asked.

"Kiana? Kiana!" Michael called her from just beneath the green and white awning of the café.

Kiana didn't turn around. She pleaded with Genevieve. The throbbing ache instantly reclaimed her head. She hadn't noticed the headache had subsided until that moment, the pain coming back tenfold. "Please, Genevieve, talk to me."

"I don't have shit to say to you." Genevieve nearly spat the words out. Her fist crunched at her small white bag. Taz glanced over her shoulder, mirrored sunglasses hiding her eyes, her full lips already turning down. She took in air and looked to Genevieve. Genevieve shook her head. "I got it, Taz. It's all right."

"Genevieve," Kiana said. "I don't understand. If I did something, just...just tell me what I did."

"Don't call me anymore. Ever." Genevieve turned and tapped Taz on the shoulder. She swung her leg up and climbed on the back of the bike.

"V! V! Whatever it was, I—" Kiana stopped. She caught herself. V. She had called her V. The motorcycle roared as it pulled away from the curb. The smoke choked Kiana where she stood. Her throat burned, and her eyes watered. She blinked, the burn intensifying and tears spilling from her eyes. Everything before her blurred. She blinked again, and it all came back. Every second of it came rushing back. Every tear. Every word. Every ache. Every touch. Every kiss. Every drink.

Every. Drink.

"Who was that?" Michael asked, walking up to Kiana. She didn't respond. He shook her shoulder. "I said, who was that? Do they know where Michelle is? Kiana, who was that?" He shook her, but she only stared at him, blinking and panting. "Kiana! Kiana!" he screamed at her face.

She snapped out of it. She wrenched herself from his grip. "I have to go," she said.

"You can't leave," Michael said. "I need your help."

Kiana shook her head. "The kind of help you need, I can't give you." She turned from him and started walking away, slowly, her entire body heavy metal, her heart fired white hot and beaten flat.

## CHAPTER NINETEEN

K iana sat at the bar. The bartender had asked her twice what he could get for her; each time, Kiana said she needed a minute. She looked across the shiny black granite and surveyed the bottles. The various shapes. The different sizes. The varying colors. Dark brown, light brown. Clear. Pale pink. Deep green. Blue. Gold.

"Made a decision? What's your poison?" the bartender asked. His blue eyes twinkling, his yellow blond hair shaggy around his ears.

Kiana looked again at the collection of bottles. She licked her lips and fidgeted with the corner of the black plastic napkin holder in front of her. Her leg bounced on the bottom of her barstool. She should just get up and leave. But she couldn't. It hurt to move. It hurt to breathe. She thought about what she had done to Genevieve. She closed her eyes and took a deep breath.

"Oh-kay," the bartender said. "I'll give you another minute." He backed away and headed to the end of the bar where a man sat sipping a shot and a beer. The two men cackled; the bartender slapped at the bar, nearly doubling over in laughter.

Kiana stared at herself in the mirror but couldn't take the sight of her own face. She glanced up at the television.

*SportsCenter*. A report on cycling. Bicycles whipping through cobbled streets, up steep mountain trails, down paved roads. She thought about her bike ride with Genevieve. The happiest moment she'd had while in New Orleans. She thought about her mother, the memory she'd had, the vision of her the bike ride conjured.

"That gentleman down there," the bartender said, walking toward her and jutting his thumb at the man at the end of the bar. "Said your drink is on him." The bartender smiled. "So, my friend, what do you want? Anything at all."

Kiana met the bartender's playful brown eyes. "I want my mama," she said.

The bartender pulled back, his face crinkling in confusion. "What is—"

Kiana raised her hand to stop him. She shook her head and pushed herself off the stool and left the bar.

## Chapter Twenty

Once inside her room, Kiana kicked off her sneakers at the door, tossed her wallet and cell phone on the nightstand, and pulled the spread off the bed. She climbed on top of the crisp white sheets and lay on her back. She stared at the ceiling and sighed. Her body, tired and still feeling heavy, welcomed the softness of the bed, the coolness of the fresh sheets.

The sun was setting, and Kiana watched the shadows in the room take shape. She closed her eyes, but sleep wouldn't come. She sat up. She looked around the room. The empty ice bucket and clean glasses on the desk caught her eye. Her flask lay on its side near the hotel services binder. She swung her legs over the side of the bed, her eyes glued to the flask. She bounced her leg and ran her hands over her hair. She picked out the back that had been flattened against the pillow. She bit at the inside of her cheek then stopped, licking her lips and sighing, all the while staring at the flask. She stood up.

At the desk, she pushed the button on the side of the lamp. A soft yellow glow illuminated the metal flask like a spotlight. It frightened her, the flask did. She was afraid to pick it up, scared that if it had booze in it, she would drink it. She nudged it with her finger. She also feared it to be empty, for if she picked it up and it was, a hope that disgusted her, but a hope all the same, would be dashed. Disappointed that the flask was empty, and even more upset at the weakness that made her check in the first place, she would collapse into the defeat of it all. She should head to the bar. A free drink was waiting. A friend waiting. She stared at the silver flask. She looked over her shoulder. It was eight o'clock. She realized she hadn't eaten all day. She hadn't been hungry, and still wasn't. She rubbed her stomach. Looking down at her arm, she noticed the smudge of metallic paint.

Kiana went into the bathroom. She turned on the faucet to wash her arm. She looked at herself in the mirror, then glanced at the floor of the bathroom, the tub, over her shoulder at the room, the carpet, the dent in the wall. Her mind couldn't focus on one thing. She stared down at the running water. She turned it off. She leaned forward, getting close enough to the mirror to see her pores, close enough that the air from her nostrils puffed against the glass, fogging it.

Fuck this, Kiana said to herself. She left the bathroom and walked past the desk, past her flask. She swiped her wallet from the nightstand but left her phone. She left the room.

❖

The elevators opened to the quiet hall. The dining room was empty. The bar, too.

"Hey, you're back," the pale-faced bartender said with a wide grin full of gray teeth. "Your patron is gone, but I'll pour you up on the house. You'll have to tell me what a 'Mama' is though. I don't know that one." He laughed.

Kiana looked in his direction but kept going, past the bar and through the dining room. She stepped up to the front desk.

"Excuse me," she said.

A woman with skin the color of coffee beans greeted her with a warm smile and gentle eyes, her navy suit and pinstriped collared shirt neat and official.

"Can I help you?" she said.

"I hope so," Kiana said. "Do you have computers for guest use? I need to book a flight."

The woman smiled. "Of course. I can help you with that," she said.

Kiana smiled back. She noticed the woman's name tag. It read "Vivien."

"Thank you, Vivien," Kiana said.

"Oh, you're welcome," Vivien said. "Let me show you to the business center." She came from behind the desk, the skirt to her suit stopping just above her shapely calves. She glanced over her shoulder, smiled, and led the way. Kiana followed close behind.

## CHAPTER TWENTY-ONE

*Sunday*

The sun crept in through the blinds, a wide stripe of light landing across Kiana's eyelids. She blinked awake and sat up. The bedside clock read ten a.m. Her flight was at six. She climbed out of bed and made her way to the bathroom. She splashed cold water on her face and met her eyes in the mirror. She looked tired, but couldn't remember the last time she had slept so soundly. She didn't remember her dreams, if she'd had any, but did remember the previous day. She remembered her evening. No gaps. No darkness. She could recall it all. Though thinking of Genevieve's expression when she had looked at her before getting on the motorcycle made her heart ache, she held on to the memory. It was a moment full of horror and shame, but she was present for it. She hadn't run away.

Kiana showered and dressed. Having run out of clothes, she pulled on the same jeans she'd worn the day before and the only semi-clean shirt she had. The blue button-up she wore to dinner at Genevieve's. She packed the rest of her things so she'd be ready to go when she got back to the hotel. Vivien, the hotel manager, had told her while helping her book her flight that she could leave her luggage behind the front desk while she took care of her last-minute business. She zipped up her bag and carried it toward the door. She stopped at the desk. Her flask, still on its side, glinted in the sunlight. She set it upright. Liquor sloshed inside as she moved it. Her hand rested on top of the screw cap. She drummed the curved body with her fingertips. She took a deep breath and held it. She teetered the flask back and forth, the sound of the whiskey inside whispering like an old lover. *Just one taste.*

Kiana blew out a sigh and rolled her shoulders. She took her hand off the flask and left it there beside the lamp. She hefted the strap of her bag onto her shoulder and left the room, closing the door softly behind her.

## CHAPTER TWENTY-TWO

The streetcar screeched to a halt. Kiana checked the stop, scanning the streets to make sure she was in the right place. She was taking one hell of a chance, but she had nothing to lose. If Genevieve was right, and there were no such thing as coincidences, then she would be there, visiting her nana as Kiana suspected. As she stepped off the streetcar, she hoped Genevieve would be willing to talk.

To her own surprise, Kiana remembered the way. She walked up the cement path, the patches of grass and sprouts of weeds bending beneath her feet. She remembered the trees, the resurrection ferns growing on their trunks, the stone crypts and monuments, the rusted gates, crumbling stone, and water stains. She came around a corner, the angel with wings solidifying her sense of direction. She heard crying. She heard Genevieve.

"No. No. No," Genevieve said when she looked up and met Kiana's eyes. She shook her head and pushed herself up from where she crouched beside her family's gravesite. She had a small white candle lit. Fresh fruit—plums, an apple, and two oranges—plopped to the ground when she stood.

"Genevieve, please," Kiana said. She held her hands out in surrender. Her voice wavered but didn't falter. "Please let me talk to you. Please listen. You owe me at least that."

Genevieve screwed her face. Her hair looked wet, the curls shiny and slick. "Owe you? Owe you? I don't owe you shit," she whispered the curse word, looking around as if she'd be scolded.

"You're right. You don't owe me anything." She still held her hands up; she slowly stepped toward Genevieve, who held her body at the ready, her knees bent like she would leap over the graves and disappear into the sky. "It's me who owes you."

Genevieve pursed her lips and raised an eyebrow. "I don't know what kind of game you're playing, but I don't have time for it. I don't want to see you. I don't want to know you. You're not welcome here." Her words stabbed Kiana.

She had no right to be offended, to be hurt. She knew that, and she was ready to face it.

"V," Kiana said.

"Don't call me that," Genevieve said. "You don't get to call me that."

Kiana dropped her hands in defeat; her chin dipped to her chest in shame and disappointment. "There is no excusing what I did to you Friday night. I'm sorrier than I've ever been in my life," she said. She looked at Genevieve, who stared back at her saying nothing.

"You don't have to accept my apology," Kiana continued. "I know that. But I had to say it. I have to be responsible for my actions."

"Your actions? What you did to me?" Genevieve laughed. She shook her head. "Get over yourself, Kiana. You didn't make me do anything. Nobody *makes* you do anything. You do what you want to do. I did what I wanted to do."

"That's not true," Kiana said. She stepped forward. Genevieve didn't back away. Kiana continued, "Friday night. I was in a bad place. The darkest place I'd ever been. I saw

Michelle for who she was that night. The way she manipulated me. The way she's always manipulated me. The way she made me—"

"Did you hear what I just said?" Genevieve said. "No one and nothing *makes* you do anything. Not Michelle. Not the alcohol. You do what you want; you do what you feel. Whether it's to escape or forget, to pity yourself or make others pity you, YOU do it. YOU DO IT!" she yelled. Her chest heaved, and she turned to catch her breath.

Kiana didn't know what to say. She thought back to what she could remember of the night. Memories mixed together, blurred and overlapped. She'd done so many things to forget. She'd done so many things to hide, to blame, to force. She'd done. She did.

"I do it," Kiana whispered. "I do it to myself." The tears came, and she didn't fight them.

Genevieve cried, too. Genevieve's shoulders shook like hers did, her breath came in sobs.

"Friday night," Genevieve said. "I chose to drink. You didn't make me." She sniffled and turned around; she wiped her eyes with the palm of her hand then crouched down to pick up the fruit that had fallen to the ground. "I've been out here all morning, talking to my nana. Trying to fill in the blanks."

Kiana walked over to Genevieve. She stood next to her and reached out to help her situate the fruit along the cement edge of the grave. Genevieve let her help.

"And?" Kiana said, setting the oranges next to each other, holding them steady so they wouldn't roll.

"Even as I told myself otherwise, I thought it was my job to save you," she said. She smirked, a tear falling before she could catch it with her wrist.

"Because of how we met?"

"Yeah. Running into you like that. It wasn't what I thought."

"But I thought you didn't believe in coincidences," Kiana said.

"It wasn't a coincidence," Genevieve said with a shrug and wry smile. "I'm never in the Quarter. When I ran into you, I ran into myself."

"I don't understand," Kiana said.

"I was there…" Genevieve paused. She took a deep breath. "I was there to get a quick drink. My first in months. It was the only place I could go where I knew I wouldn't run into anyone who knew me, who knew my nana, who knew that I had…sobered up." Genevieve looked at Kiana and smiled, her warm, honey eyes sparkling with clarity. "I was hurting and feeling alone."

"I'm confused," Kiana said. She sat in the grass beside Nana's grave. She glanced at the stone etching. *I AM NOT GONE.* The words didn't scare her like before. They comforted her.

Genevieve sat beside her. "Don't be," she said.

"I'm saying though," Kiana sighed. "I came to apologize and…what does all this mean?"

"It means," Genevieve said, "that we both needed this. It means we found each other." She pulled her legs up under her and stared straight ahead.

Kiana bumped her shoulder against Genevieve's, taking a deep breath and looking at the sky. Silence passed between them. Thunder rumbled in the distance, and rain, cool and life-affirming, dropped down from the heavy gray clouds. Kiana didn't move. She kept her face turned to the sky, fat drops of water splashing against her forehead and cheeks. She exhaled and turned to Genevieve.

"I'm Kiana, and I'm an alcoholic," she said. She looked at Genevieve, who turned to face her, squinting against the gentle rain.

"Hi, Kiana. I'm Genevieve, and I'm an alcoholic." She wiped her hand on her jeans and offered it to Kiana. "It's nice to meet you. My friends call me 'V.'"

Kiana took her hand and shook it. "Nice to meet you, too, V."

They shook again, a firm grip that lingered after the shaking, after the introductions. Kiana held Genevieve's hand, and Genevieve held hers. The rain continued to fall, making moist what had been dry, restoring life to what seemed to be dead.

Kiana closed her eyes and remembered the strength, the comfort of Karyn's hands. Karyn's warm palm, the way her fingers linked with hers during their mother's funeral. Karyn's hand dangling loose and carefree as she draped her arm around Kiana's shoulders as they walked to the bus stop. Karyn stroking her hair lovingly when she woke up from nightmares, pressing her palm against Kiana's forehead when she felt sick. Karyn rubbing soft circles at the small of her back when Kiana cried over her first girlfriend. Karyn's hand reaching for the steering wheel when she taught her to drive. Her hands lifting and pushing boxes; Karyn's fingers curling into a fist as she joked and showed off her biceps while helping Kiana move into her first apartment. Karyn's hand reaching across the car to unlock the door when she picked her up, lonely and afraid, from the 69th street Redline stop.

Kiana glanced at the inscription once more. *I AM NOT GONE.* She looked at Genevieve's hand clasping hers and thought again of Karyn's hands. Her sister's hands, which were her mother's hands, hands that were always there.

## CHAPTER TWENTY-THREE

Kiana dug her phone out of her pocket as she made her way to the escalator. She held her Chicago Card against the sensor and pushed through the turnstile. Gliding down the escalator to the train, she called Karyn.

"Kiana!" Karyn said, loud and fast.

"Yeah," Kiana said. "I'm home."

"You were supposed to tell me when you landed so I could pick you up. Who did you fly in with? You at O'Hare or Midway? What terminal?" Karyn rambled on, at the ready as always. Kiana heard the click of her heels on the hardwoods, the shuffle of her slipping on her jacket, the swipe of keys from the cocktail table.

"Slow down, slow down," Kiana said. "I flew into O'Hare, but I'm getting on the train."

"Don't get on the train."

"I'm getting on the train. It's fine." Kiana stepped off the escalator and adjusted her bag on her shoulder. "I would appreciate it if you scooped me from downtown though."

"Are you all right?" Karyn asked. The screen door creaked and slammed shut.

"I'm great," Kiana said. "A little jet-lagged, but I'm good."

"You sound different." Wind whooshed against the receiver. It stopped abruptly with the slam of the car door.

"Good different or bad different?" Kiana said.

"I'm not sure," Karyn said. She jingled the keys and started her car. The seat belt indicator beep sounded off, the radio coming to life. "Say something else," she said.

Kiana laughed. She walked toward the train, readjusting her bag on her shoulder. She boarded behind a brown-haired couple with hard case valises.

"Hold on a second. I need to find a seat." Kiana maneuvered around several other people with their luggage. She settled on a window seat near the doors. "What were you saying?" Kiana said.

"I was saying you sounded different, but I couldn't decide if it was good different or bad different," Karyn repeated.

"I hope good different," Kiana said. She looked out the window as the train pulled off. "I haven't had a drink in two days. Maybe that's it."

"Two days?" Karyn said, a hint of mocking in her voice. She started to laugh then stopped. "I'm sorry."

"It's okay," Kiana said. "It's just two days." She shrugged.

"It's not just two days, Kiana," Karyn said. "It's a start."

"Yeah," Kiana said. "It's a start." Karyn agreed to meet her at the Jackson stop. She ended the call and slid her phone into the front zip of her bag. She glanced up at the Blue Line map though she knew the route frontward and backward. Smiling, Kiana settled into her seat, grateful to finally be moving forward.

# About the Author

A Milwaukee, Wisconsin, native, Sheree L. Greer has been published in *Hair Trigger*, *The Windy City Times*, *Reservoir*, *Fictionary*, *The Windy City Queer Anthology: Dispatches from the Third Coast*, and *Best Lesbian Romance 2012*. She has performed her work across selected venues in Milwaukee, New York, Miami, Chicago, and Tampa, where she hosts Oral Fixation, the only LGBTQ Open Mic series in Tampa Bay. She earned her MFA at Columbia College Chicago and currently teaches writing and literature at St. Petersburg College. Sheree, an Astraea Lesbian Writers Fund grantee, completed a VONA residency at University of Miami and self-published a short story collection, *Once and Future Lovers*.

While her obsessions constantly rotate and evolve, Sheree has an undying love for hot sauces, red wines, and crunchy tacos. She plays less-than-mediocre electric guitar but makes nearly-perfect guacamole.

# Books Available From Bold Strokes Books

**Let the Lover Be** by Sheree Greer. Kiana Lewis, a functional alcoholic on the verge of destruction, finally faces the demons of her past while finding love and earning redemption in New Orleans. (978-1-62639-077-5)

**Blindsided** by Karis Walsh. Blindsided by love, guide dog trainer Lenae McIntyre and media personality Cara Bradley learn to trust what they see with their hearts. (978-1-62639-078-2)

**About Face** by VK Powell. Forensic artist Macy Sheridan and Detective Leigh Monroe work on a case that has troubled them both for years, but they're hampered by the past and their unlikely yet undeniable attraction. (978-1-62639-079-9)

**Blackstone** by Shea Godfrey. For Darry and Jessa, their chance at a life of freedom is stolen by the arrival of war and an ancient prophecy that just might destroy their love. (978-1-62639-080-5)

**Out of This World** by Maggie Morton. Iris decided to cross an ocean to get over her ex. But instead, she ends up traveling much farther, all the way to another world. Once there, only a mysterious, sexy, and magical woman can help her return home. (978-1-62639-083-6)

**Kiss The Girl** by Melissa Brayden. Sleeping with the enemy has never been so complicated. Brooklyn Campbell and Jessica Lennox face off in love and advertising in fast-paced New York City. (978-1-62639-071-3)

**Taking Fire: A First Responders Novel** by Radclyffe. Hunted by extremists and under siege by nature's most virulent weapons, Navy medic Max de Milles and Red Cross worker Rachel Winslow join forces to survive and discover something far more lasting. (978-1-62639-072-0)

**First Tango in Paris** by Shelley Thrasher. When French law student Eva Laroche meets American call girl Brigitte Green in 1970s Paris, they have no idea how their pasts and futures will intersect. (978-1-62639-073-7)

**The War Within** by Yolanda Wallace. Army nurse Meredith Moser went to Vietnam in 1967 looking to help those in need; she didn't expect to meet the love of her life along the way. (978-1-62639-074-4)

**Escapades** by MJ Williamz. Two women, afraid to love again, must overcome their fears to find the happiness that awaits them. (978-1-62639-182-6)

**Desire at Dawn** by Fiona Zedde. For Kylie, love had always come armed with sharp teeth and claws. But with the human, Olivia, she bares her vampire heart for the very first time, sharing passion, lust, and a tenderness she'd never dared dream of before. (978-1-62639-064-5)

**Visions** by Larkin Rose. Sometimes the mysteries of love reveal themselves when you least expect it. Other times they hide behind a black satin mask. Can Paige unveil her masked stranger this time? (978-1-62639-065-2)

**All In** by Nell Stark. Internet poker champion Annie Navarro loses everything when the Feds shut down online gambling, and she turns to experienced casino host Vesper Blake for advice—but can Nova convince Vesper to take a gamble on romance? (978-1-62639-066-9)

**Vermilion Justice** by Sheri Lewis Wohl. What's a vampire to do when Dracula is no longer just a character in a novel? (978-1-62639-067-6)

**Switchblade** by Carsen Taite. Lines were meant to be crossed. Third in the Luca Bennett Bounty Hunter Series. (978-1-62639-058-4)

**Nightingale** by Andrea Bramhall. Culture, faith, and duty conspire to tear two young lovers apart, yet fate seems to have different plans for them both. (978-1-62639-059-1)

**No Boundaries** by Donna K. Ford. A chance meeting and a nightmare from the past threaten more than Andi Massey's solitude as she and Gwen Palmer struggle to understand the complexity of love without boundaries. (978-1-62639-060-7)

**Timeless** by Rachel Spangler. When Stevie Geller returns to her hometown, will she do things differently the second time around or will she be in such a hurry to leave her past that she misses out on a better future? (978-1-62639-050-8)

**Second to None** by L.T. Marie. Can a physical therapist and a custom motorcycle designer conquer their pasts and build a future with one another? (978-1-62639-051-5)

**Seneca Falls** by Jesse Thoma. Together, two women discover love truly can conquer all evil. (978-1-62639-052-2)

**A Kingdom Lost** by Barbara Ann Wright. Without knowing each other's fates, Princess Katya and her consort Starbride seek to reclaim their kingdom from the magic-wielding madman who seized the throne and is murdering their people. (978-1-62639-053-9)

**Season of the Wolf** by Robin Summers. Two women running from their pasts are thrust together by an unimaginable evil. Can they overcome the horrors that haunt them in time to save each other? (978-1-62639-043-0)

**The Heat of Angels** by Lisa Girolami. Fires burn in more than one place in Los Angeles. (978-1-62639-042-3)

**Desperate Measures** by P. J. Trebelhorn. Homicide detective Kay Griffith and contractor Brenda Jansen meet amidst turmoil neither of them is aware of until murder suspect Tommy Rayne makes his move to exact revenge on Kay. (978-1-62639-044-7)

**The Magic Hunt** by L.L. Raand. With her Pack being hunted by human extremists and beset by enemies masquerading as friends, can Sylvan protect them and her mate, or will she succumb to the feral rage that threatens to turn her rogue, destroying them all? A Midnight Hunters novel. (978-1-62639-045-4)

**Wingspan** by Karis Walsh. Wildlife biologist Bailey Chase is content to live at the wild bird sanctuary she has created on Washington's Olympic Peninsula until she is lured beyond the safety of isolation by architect Kendall Pearson. (978-1-60282-983-1)

**Windigo Thrall** by Cate Culpepper. Six women trapped in a mountain cabin by a blizzard, stalked by an ancient cannibal demon bent on stealing their sanity—and their lives. (978-1-60282-950-3)

**The Blush Factor** by Gun Brooke. Ice-cold business tycoon Eleanor Ashcroft only cares about the three Ps—Power, Profit, and Prosperity—until young Addison Garr makes her doubt both that and the state of her frostbitten heart. (978-1-60282-985-5)

**Slash and Burn** by Valerie Bronwen. The murder of a roundly despised author at an LGBT writers' conference in New Orleans turns Winter Lovelace's relaxing weekend hobnobbing with her peers into a nightmare of suspense—especially when her ex turns up. (978-1-60282-986-2)

**The Quickening: A Sisters of Spirits Novel** by Yvonne Heidt. Ghosts, visions, and demons are all in a day's work for Tiffany. But when Kat asks for help on a serial killer case, life takes on another dimension altogether. (978-1-60282-975-6)

**Smoke and Fire** by Julie Cannon. Oil and water, passion and desire, a combustible combination. Can two women fight the fire that draws them together and threatens to keep them apart? (978-1-60282-977-0)

**Love and Devotion** by Jove Belle. KC Hall trips her way through life, stumbling into an affair with a married bombshell twice her age. Thankfully, her best friend, Emma Reynolds, is there to show her the true meaning of Love and Devotion. (978-1-60282-965-7)


**The Shoal of Time** by J.M. Redmann. It sounded too easy. Micky Knight is reluctant to take the case because the easy ones often turn into the hard ones, and the hard ones turn into the dangerous ones. In this one, easy turns hard without warning. (978-1-60282-967-1)